Catchin' the Drift o' the Draft

Books by LOUIS DANIEL BRODSKY

Poetry

Five Facets of Myself   (1967)* (1995)

The Easy Philosopher   (1967)* (1995)

"A Hard Coming of It" and Other Poems   (1967)* (1995)

The Foul Rag-and-Bone Shop   (1967)* (1969)* (1995)

Points in Time   (1971)* (1995) (1996)

Taking the Back Road Home   (1972)* (1997)

Trip to Tipton and Other Compulsions   (1973)* (1997)

"The Talking Machine" and Other Poems   (1974)* (1997)

Tiffany Shade   (1974)* (1997)

Trilogy: A Birth Cycle   (1974) (1998)

Cold Companionable Streams   (1975)* (1999)

Monday's Child   (1975) (1998)

Preparing for Incarnations   (1975)* (1976) (1999) (1999 exp.)

The Kingdom of Gewgaw   (1976)

Point of Americas II   (1976) (1998)

La Preciosa   (1977)

Stranded in the Land of Transients   (1978)

The Uncelebrated Ceremony of Pants Factory Fatso   (1978)

Birds in Passage   (1980)

Résumé of a Scrapegoat   (1980)

Mississippi Vistas: Volume One of *A Mississippi Trilogy*   (1983) (1990)

You Can't Go Back, Exactly   (1988) (1988) (1989)

The Thorough Earth   (1989)

Four and Twenty Blackbirds Soaring   (1989)

Falling from Heaven: Holocaust Poems of a Jew and a Gentile
   (with William Heyen)   (1991)

Forever, for Now: Poems for a Later Love   (1991)

Mistress Mississippi: Volume Three of *A Mississippi Trilogy*   (1992)

A Gleam in the Eye: Poems for a First Baby   (1992)

Gestapo Crows: Holocaust Poems   (1992)

The Capital Café: Poems of Redneck, U.S.A.   (1993)

Disappearing in Mississippi Latitudes: Volume Two of *A Mississippi
   Trilogy*   (1994)

A Mississippi Trilogy: A Poetic Saga of the South   (1995)*

Paper-Whites for Lady Jane: Poems of a Midlife Love Affair   (1995)

The Complete Poems of Louis Daniel Brodsky: Volume One, 1963–1967
   (edited by Sheri L. Vandermolen)   (1996)

Three Early Books of Poems by Louis Daniel Brodsky, 1967–1969: *The Easy Philosopher*, *"A Hard Coming of It" and Other Poems*, and *The Foul Rag-and-Bone Shop* *(edited by Sheri L. Vandermolen)*   (1997)

The Eleventh Lost Tribe: Poems of the Holocaust   (1998)

Toward the Torah, Soaring: Poems of the Renascence of Faith   (1998)

Bibliography (Coedited with Robert Hamblin)

Selections from the William Faulkner Collection of Louis Daniel Brodsky: A Descriptive Catalogue   (1979)

Faulkner: A Comprehensive Guide to the Brodsky Collection
    Volume I: The Bibliography   (1982)
    Volume II: The Letters   (1984)
    Volume III: *The De Gaulle Story*   (1984)
    Volume IV: *Battle Cry*   (1985)
    Volume V: Manuscripts and Documents   (1989)

Country Lawyer and Other Stories for the Screen by William Faulkner   (1987)

Stallion Road: A Screenplay by William Faulkner   (1989)

Biography

William Faulkner, Life Glimpses   (1990)

Fiction

The Adventures of the Night Riders, Better Known as the Terrible Trio *(with Richard Milsten)*   (1961)[*]

Between Grief and Nothing   (1964)[*]

Between the Heron and the Wren   (1965)[*]

Dink Phlager's Alligator *(novella)*   (1966)[*]

The Drift of Things   (1966)[*]

Vineyard's Toys   (1967)[*]

The Bindlestiffs   (1968)[*]

Yellow Bricks   (1999)

Catchin' the Drift o' the Draft   (1999)

This Here's a Merica   (1999)

[*] *Unpublished*

Catchin' the Drift o' the Draft

Short fictions

by

L.D. Brodsky

TIME BEING BOOKS

POETRY IN SIGHT AND SOUND

St. Louis, Missouri

Time Being Books®
10411 Clayton Road
St. Louis, Missouri 63131

Time Being Books® is an imprint of Time Being Press®
St. Louis, Missouri

Time Being Press® is a 501(c)(3) not-for-profit corporation.

Time Being Books® volumes are printed on acid-free paper, and binding materials are chosen for strength and durability.

The characters and events portrayed in these stories are fictitious. Any similarities to real persons, living or dead, is purely coincidental and not intended by the author.

ISBN 1-56809-052-8 (Paperback)

Library of Congress Cataloging-in-Publication Data:

Brodsky, Louis Daniel.
    Catchin' the drift o' the draft : short fictions / by L.D. Brodsky. — 1st ed.
      p.   cm.
   ISBN 1-56809-052-8 (pbk. : alk. paper)
   1. United States—Social life and customs—20th century Fiction.   I. Title.
PS3552.R623C38   1999
  813'.54—dc21   99-24791
                                                CIP

Book design and typesetting by Sheri L. Vandermolen
Manufactured in the United States of America

First Edition, first printing (1999)

Acknowledgments

Jerry Call, Editor in Chief of Time Being Books, encouraged me to develop these fictions into a full-fledged collection. I owe him much for his devotion to helping me make this volume a gratifying reality.

Sheri L. Vandermolen, Senior Editor of Time Being Books, read these pieces with an uncommonly astute critical eye. Without her skill to guide me, this book would never have approximated my ultimate vision for it.

For Jerry Call,

who, as my editor,
shares with me the belief
that satire, the surreal, and hyperbole
pick up where martyrs leave off,

if you catch my drift.

Contents

Dumbfounded *17*

Monday Night Football *19*

On the Curious Affinity of Triangles, Circles, and Squares *20*

A Postlude to Thanksgivin' *22*

Long-Term Memory *26*

Horses of a Different Color *27*

Dr. Johnson Spends Christmas Eve Alone in His Cups *29*

Working the Graveyard Shift *30*

A Thing for Red *32*

'Twas the Day After Xmas *33*

The Rehabilitation of a War Criminal *37*

Going Ape *38*

Dreaming of Dying in the Saddle *40*

In Defense of the Nation's Honor *42*

Paradise Endangered *43*

The Men's Sodality Convenes at Redbird's *45*

The Walking Dead *47*

Warehouse of Mannequins *49*

Boomlay, Boom *50*

Harry Carpin, Deliveryman *52*

Back to Normal *53*

Shall Rise Again *54*

Regnum Christi *55*

A Small Investor *59*

The Vanity of Human Delusions *61*

My Life as an Egg Beater *63*

Chronic Absenteeism *64*

Planet of the Prime Apes *65*

Death's Bridegroom *67*

All Greeks to Me *69*

Professor Emeritus of Western Civilization *73*

J.C.'s San Francisco Reverie *74*

Ship of Fools *77*

A Mama's Boy *79*

A Day in the Life of a Nightmare *81*

Hell o' Dolly *82*

Fear and Trembling *87*

Sepulture in February *89*

Not the Only Gamester in Town *90*

Ringing in Spring Clichés *92*

There Goes the Neighborhood *95*

Catchin' the Drift o' the Draft

Dumbfounded

What a strange sensation occurred last week. I awakened as if in a dream-amnesia, that dislocation we frequently experience when surfacing from the nightmarish depths of turbulent sleep, knotted and clotted with seaweed and jagged reefs graffitied with images and slogans threatening, inhumane, unholy, obscene.

My body was covered with blood, though I couldn't see it smeared all over my flesh. Most disturbing was my loss of words; literally, I had no reservoir of them from which to draw to describe my condition to ghosts at bedside, keeping an occult candlelight vigil. It's one thing, I imagine, to go slowly deaf, blind, but to have one's entire lexicon deleted is a defeat of the spirit too frightening to believe and, it goes without saying, impossible to articulate.

For hours, I hid beneath the sheets, strained my vocal cords, stretched my tongue, breathed out and in like a bellows to ignite certain sounds, hoping to rekindle the beginning of syllables, whose logical accretion might render words, phrases, sentences containing fundamental pleas for expedient help. Even yelling and screaming refused to materialize, until, finally, I realized I'd been condemned to silence; for what reason I yet had no clue.

True, over my thirty years as an obsessed professional poet, I've been accused of abusing the mother tongue with tortured, convoluted syntax depending on polysyllabic vocabulary for its intricacies. But style is a personal preference, and I've always assumed that freedom of choice was a virtue, a human entitlement. After all, weren't Shakespeare, Milton, Swift, Carlyle, Melville, and Faulkner haughty practitioners of high-blown rhetoric, achieving feats with the English language never before conceived? Why should I be made to suffer, even if such were the cause of my curious malady?

Now, it's five days later. My body is growing emaciated from hunger; my throat is raspy and painful. My sheets reek of urine; I'm coated with feces. Yet I refuse to leave this bed, this room, knowing I can't speak. What to do? What indeed will happen to me if this persists one more week? Truth is, I've lost the strength even to raise myself, lift my arm to reach for pen and pad, not that it would matter. Exorcising demons depends to a great extent on verbalizing demands, drafting releases to be signed by the enemy, and these require words spoken and written — words, words, those precious instruments without which we can't defend ourselves, even from ourselves.

What will come of me in the days ahead as this curse worsens and expression diminishes to twitching lips, numb tongue, memory forgetting itself? Even my stifled cries of self-pity will be squandered on death, that loquacious bastard who never lets anyone get a word in edgewise.

Monday Night Football

For reasons clear even to his overloaded psyche, he could sense a rout on the way as early as the initial four series of downs, in which one team fumbled twice, giving up a field goal first, followed by an undefensed embarrassment: a sixty-five-yard pass play to a rogue halfback, which flashed seven more points on the board.

And that was that for his patience, the end of the beginning of a relaxing evening, the beginning of a painful end to a day's torment, which he normally controlled with three hours of mindless action and a few brews, maybe a six-pack.

Switching channels with his remote like a magician waving a wand over a hat to transfigure scarves into a rainbow of birds, he metamorphosed *Monday Night Football* into Maya Angelou pontificating about Giotto, then into *The Whole Story of Adolf Hitler*, a study of the *Führer*'s profligacies as an art student in Vienna, through his heroic gassing in WWI, to his appropriation of the role of chancellor, his grandiose delusions glorified to their gory denouement.

But neither the Renaissance nor the Third Reich satisfied his restive spirit. Frantically, he began to run the gamut of channels, until he landed, like a roulette ball in a winning slot, on Cinemax, where three naked lesbians were engaged in cunnilingus so provocative he broke into nervous laughter, not sure whether he should feel aroused or repulsed.

Never before had he set aside a beer. His earlobes began to sweat, then his upper lip. Within minutes, he'd unzipped his pants, crescendoing toward his Zenith of vicarious pleasure.

Supine and spent, he reactivated the remote, left the odalisques to their clitoral titillations, flashed past the mustachioed, goose-stepping psychopath, past the black talking head, and arrived back at the football game just in time to see a quarterback gurneyed to the locker room, a fitting climax to another Monday night.

On the Curious Affinity
of Triangles, Circles, and Squares

While researching facts for a law brief assigned to him by the Supreme Court justice for whom he clerks, his eyes inadvertently strayed, out of boredom, indolence, or frustration, from the *World Book* volume he was using (what he was doing relying on this source of information was unfathomable to him in the first place and not a little disturbing for its suggestion of an early stage of some mental disorder) to another, with an article classifying triangles, as though focusing on these shapes might somehow relieve tension or lead him to an elusive conclusion about racism, bigotry, prejudice, and discrimination he'd not previously contemplated.

But just letting his lips silently articulate the types, then whispering their strange names — terminology as abstruse as Linnaean taxonomy (obtuse, acute, oblique, right, equilateral, isosceles) — he suddenly realized that while the angles of each triangle were confined, on the inside, to 180 degrees, the sum of their outside rotations amounted to 360, the identical number in a circle and square.

Perhaps it was not mere coincidence that equated the geometry of disparate images but design foreordained, predestined. Whatever the case, he spent the next two hours in the library, drawing various shapes on legal paper to see if he could discover esoteric relationships among the forms his imagination rendered from memory — whose memory and of what, he couldn't say — until he seemingly exhausted all possibilities and was again ready to concentrate on the nuances of *Brown v. Board of Education*.

But when he tried to bolster his argument in favor of desegregation and Affirmative Action, he couldn't remember any of the axioms or theories that constituted the foundation of his LL.D., and he began to doubt the wisdom of his decision to pursue a career in jurisprudence, in civil-tort reform, furthering humanitarian goals.

How a triangle, circle, and square could be equal in any way, if not shape or form, he could only accept on faith, and he'd been taught that belief in things unseen yielded circumstantial evidence through whose bored-out mountainside you could drive two locomotives at the same time.

Thoroughly confused, he closed the encyclopedia, took leave of the moldy library, and returned to the office, where later that same day he would submit his resignation, clear his desk, and disappear.

A Postlude to Thanksgivin'

It mine as well o' been the Last Supper as Thanksgivin', if you catch the drift o' my draft. I took three bites, turned around, and we was outten sight, gone with the dust, if you catch the drift o' my wind. Truth is, I couldn't eat none o' that stuff noways. Whoever done heard o' servin' beast tendon-loins, boneless bonered ham, waxed 'n wanin' beans, 'n baby taters 'n tots on turkey day? Jeezus!

Yeah, that's what my old lady's brother done cooked up. I mean, where did he think he was, Rooskia, Bozoslobovia, Pay-go Pay-go, Sand Francisco Cove? Jeezus, this here's a national holiday — Pilgrins, Indials, cramberry-can mold, candy-ass yams, hatchets, TV parades, gimlets 'n gravy, oyster loafs, stove-topped dressin', pigskin matches up the wazoo, succulent breast-meats o' patriotic gobbler, if you catch the tits o' my tats — froth Thursday of every November! I mean, before 'n after all, this here's a Merica!

So we don't stay more'n a hour or so, visitin' 'n drinkin' up 'n downin' their brews, but not even eight seconds of eatin' before we beg off, me makin' the excuse that the missus got her red tide, the menstruable cycle, you know, on the raggy Ann 'n Andy, complete with all the fixin's: headsnake, gas up the ass, that cold, damp feelin' she hates down her leg — above all, the nastiest cramps this side o' the Missus-Sloppy — oh, and don't let me forget, one real bitchy outlook on life 'n me too that lasts every bit o' twenty-eight hours a day, goin' on three days minimal, give or take a month o' Mondays 'n then some. We may o' hurt their feelin's some, but there's situationals you just gotta stick by your pistols, stomp your feet down, refuse to give out when it comes to givin' in to principals 'n other long-standin' persons of aliment'ry authority.

So we ditch their house. I'm starvin' like a skeleton, and we drive to the first Bob Evans we see, 'cause Stompanato's ain't open, which is a real bummer, and Fubar's, which is — open, that is — is off limits, 'cause my old lady said so. At Bob's, they're runnin' a "Plymouth Rock Special" (they got rubber turkeys, like cuckoonuts on palmed trees, hangin' from where they usually got hangin' the Confederal 'n Canadial flags o' the U.S. of A. and billboards throwed up just for the day all over the outside 'n windows, sayin' "ALL YOU CARE TO EAT" about ten times to hell, so's, natch, the highway's jammed up with axledents from rubberneckers gawkin' at all them rubber turkeys 'n such, so's, natch, the powers o' suggestibles didn't have to work too goddamn hard to pull me in neither), and I know we can tie on a "ALL YOU CARE TO EAT" feed bag for under six boy-Georges apiece, includin' all the trimmin's 'n fixin's 'n such, which makes me feel even less bad leavin' a freebie behind, even if I done so purely on principals. And was that *some* feast! Everything but the wattlers! What in hell's the missus's brother think Thanksgivin's all about, anyways — that wishboners grow on cows, pigs sprout drumsticks outten their snouts?

So's I wattle into Redbird's, this Monday mornin', after snoozin' through a Ripped Van Tinkle weekend o' pure 'n unadulteried pigskinizations by all five major 'n minor nutworks simultaneously at the same time, which made it almost impossomable to not keep from gettin' the pros mixed up with the collegials (me pullin' for New England's Fightin' Irish against Neuter Dame's Patrials, the New Orleans Menstruable Tides against Bama's Crimson Saints), which didn't matter to me noways, since somethin' in Bob Evans' turkey done put me to sleep over 'n below the normal affects o' my brewskies.

Truth is, the fack I can wattle right now at all is attribute to my pure 'n unadulteral love for the work I do, 'cause in about forty-five minutes, I'm supposed to show up on the assemblage line out to Saturn 69 and give a big heil-five to Alferneeze "Geez, Cain't See Ma Knees" Johnson and pretend like this is just like any other ol' normal run-o'-the-general-mills Monday mornin', instead o' the aftermast o' Thanksgivin', which, suddlenly I realize, it *is*, since Redbird's stinks to high hell like a poultry-renderin' stocked yard over to East St. Louis or Sauget, with the odorization o' turkey hash 'n turkey ham 'n turkey-fried steaks 'n turkey omlits 'n turkey taters 'n turkey noodle soup 'n turkey veggie burgers on turkey buns 'n Belchum turkey waffles with turkey wallnuts 'n turkey powder sugar, upside-down- turkey pineapple cakes 'n turkey cuckoonut cream pies 'n turkey coffee — Jeezus, even Traci 'n Gert 'n Harriet stink to high shit, like they been out back, pullin' feathers 'n choppin' necks 'n wings 'n legs all night to throw into the vat Cookie's got boilin' to beat all hell!

I mean, after all, what do you do with the leftovers when you've used up all the leftover shit you can use in the turkey-salad sammiches 'n turkey loafs 'n potted turkey pies 'n still got enough leftovers left over to send home with the help 'n offer to the winos 'n homeless down to Reverend Soulard's New Shinin' Light o' Hope 'n Envy Mission o' Knights o' the River Michael Jordan 'n still got enough to fill a thousand carry-out dog bags to give all us regulars who ain't already stuffed to their gulls, as a compumentary-on-the-house-gradus tokens o' their steam for us bein' such loyal patronages?

Jeezus! I'm *so* fuckin' *sick* o' **TURKEY** I could blow a entire Butterball outten my ass the entire length o' Redbird's main dinin' facility, which ain't all that big a dangerous deal anyways, really, since it'd prob'ly hit one o' them fat Cathlick mackerel snappers square in the chops (and he'd swallow it so fuckin' fast no one'd even be the wiser to where it landed) before it'd ever bust through the plate-glass window and land smack-dab-for-splatter in the middle o' Hydraulic 'n Botanical, snarlin' traffic worse than it ever was over to the highway by Bob Evans that suckered me 'n the missus in in the first place, goddamnit, with them rubber turkeys squawkin' from their flagpoles, "ALL YOU CARE TO EAT! ALL YOU CARE TO EAT! ALL YOU CARE TO EAT!"

In fack, come to think on it, I wish to shit we done stayed over to her brother's and had a unnormal feast o' beast tendonloins 'n bonered ham 'n waxed 'n wanin' beans 'n baby taters 'n tots, 'cause I ain't usually got no problems makin' Monday mornin' if all Monday mornin' is is pigskin leftovers; but turkey leftovers is a horse of another suit altogether, guarangoddamnteeya!

Long-Term Memory

Each morning, in his sprawling nursing home, he tries to come to terms with who he'll be when he no longer remembers yesterday. Already, he forgets within seconds having eaten breakfast — what food he's had, by whom he was spoon-fed — despite still experiencing glimmers of youth, traces of escapades from adolescence, montages of his adult life — family, career, philanthropic deeds.

What most intimidates him is the prospect of his synapses snapping, their lines of communication crackling with cacophonous static, hissing masses of Alzheimer's wires abandoning him to a dark arctic glacier, where he'll float alone, irreversibly comatose.

Whose identity will then own him remains to be ascertained, that impasse looming so near he can almost hear himself disappearing even as he chews a sliver of honeydew melon his tongue misconstrues for his bleeding gums, which he believes are being massaged by a nurse he's certain is his rosy-cheeked mother feeding him zwieback in his highchair, eighty-odd eons ago to the nanosecond.

Horses of a Different Color

The laws of the land, Houyhnhnmland, had grown cumbersome and arcane, effete, if not completely irrelevant, under the reign of Bucephalus, Chief Justice of the Supreme Equine Court. They no longer seemed to serve the needs of the greatest number of its citizens, rather pandered only to the few elite, who had themselves grown cumbersome and arcane, bloated with their own self-importance as horses with enough clout to fix the human race annually, indeterminately, ensuring their own bloody fortunes by betting on the ever-changing entrants in the ever-present running of whatever Triple Crown might be in town.

They'd grown sated with their authority, swollen on their oats and sugar, vegetative, until, despite their totalitarian control, they foundered, splay-legged, began dying in droves, like sheep (a demeaning fate, at best), in herds, like lowly beef cattle (an even more degrading humiliation), collapsing as though decimated by anthrax, relying on mere people to succor them, provide the model and means of euthanasia, the pervasive examples of suicide, homicide, genocide humans employed to improve their condition, make room for Malthusian and Hitlerian *Übermenschen*, to relieve them in their lemminglike expiration. (Oh, the shame of the whole cataclysm, that all their nobility and glory should have devolved to this, a diminishment and surrender and corruption not even worthy of humans!)

Now, the laws of the land, Houyhnhnmland, are the stuff of legend, myth, fable, parable, of a long-ago and faraway time and place in which horses of all manner ruled the planet, from the granddaddy of them all, the sixteen-toed Eohippus, to Appaloosas, Morgans, and Arabians; Belgians, Clydesdales, Percherons, Suffolks, and Shires; albinos, pintos, and palominos; tarpans, Lipizzaners, and Przewalski's horses; ponies (Welshes, Shetlands, Hackneys, Connemaras), nags, plugs, hacks, jades, crowbaits, and scalawags; balkers, jugheads, rogues, rackaboneses, and scrags; their hybridized, domesticated, and mutated cousins (donkeys [jacks and jennies], mules and hinnies); onagers of ancient times, lesser related aberrations and offshoots (zebras, hippos [river horses], Malayan tapirs), legendary steeds and mounts (the famished Black Horse of the Apocalypse; Incitatus, the wino priest and consul of Caligula; Rocinante, the "Don"'s majestic bag o' bones; Sleipnir, Odin's eight-legged amphibian; Xanthus, the pissed-off prophet of Achilles' demise; the Trojan Horse, the Grecian woody with wheels; Clever Hans, the calculating colt; Francis, the loquacious ass; Mr. Ed — of course, of course!), and winged and horned beasts as well (Pegasus, Al Borak, unicorns in abundance, and mares of night and day).

Today, only a trace of those sleek, hoofed quadrupeds remains, one grotesque and dwarfish distortion: Wolfgang, a nine-hundred-year-old Shetland pony, measuring half a hand high by five inches from tip of tail to maneless head, who roams the land, in a cage (tended by the reincarnation of Amadeus Mozart's sister, nicknamed "Horseface" by her brother, "Wolfie"), an anomaly that has barely drawn enough audience for the last few centuries to pay for the traveling entourage and menagerie of one. And no one in the Kingdom of Things, formerly Houyhnhnmland, even believes, anymore, that once upon a dream, Bucephalus reigned supreme, when today's rulers were odious little vermin, Yahoos, no more than stableboys, Kapos, attendants to the greatest race of creatures ever to exist, instead of theologians, philosophers, doctors, scientists, poets, politicians, and systems analysts known and respected, above all, for their horse sense, that vestige which yet indebts them to their glorious origins.

Dr. Johnson Spends Christmas Eve Alone in His Cups

Christmas Eve has caught me up short, with my pants down, two quarts low, one oar out of the water, four sandwiches shy of a picnic, tattooed and screwed blue, you might say, if you weren't trying to be literal but figurative, lateral, literate, clitoral, collateral, syllogistic, solipsistic, narcissistic, pessimistic, pissed.

Truth is, 'tis the season to commit folly, run outdoors naked and sing wassails with neighbors, get crocked on English eggnog, Irish grog, Scottish bog-tipple bitters, slog home to the missus and kids, and set up a feast by the chimney for the jolly red giant, his rotundity, St. Nick, hoping he doesn't get stuck like a cork in a bottle of fine Madeira wine.

Ah, but I digress. Tonight is the big megillah, the shining hour, the whole nine yards, the full bull, Santa's Candyland, Canaan, and *Cannabis sativa* all rolled up into one jubilee doobie, an epiphany for atheists, agnostics, and faithful alike.

Trouble is, I have no family, tree, gifts, no reason to be cheerful, joyous, euphoric, abstemious. Three bahs and a humbug! Amen!

Working the Graveyard Shift

Lately, in that sleep zone dividing noon from 10 p.m., in which he performs death's dress rehearsals, he's been sighting breaching green leviathans on the horizon, having the crew of the ghost whaler he captains, the good ship *Hallucination*, lower him overboard in a dory fitted with harpoon rigging, so that, alone, he might maneuver within shooting distance and take his chances on single-handedly killing one to prove to his inexorably shrinking manhood, that indeed he's still worthy of outsized deeds, not just the menial tasks he's assigned at the factory or the even more humiliating chores his wife of forty years devises to neuter him when he returns home for breakfast, bedraggled and forlorn.

But he has yet to rise at ten in the evening with the slightest trace of evidence — an eyeball, bloody chunk of blubber, plate from a baleen — to place in a formaldehyde-filled jar he might set on the mantel, stare at when he lapses, reading the morning paper in the easy chair to which he habitually retires to escape for a fleeting while from the wife he knows sooner than soon will contentiously invent some useless duty she'll accuse him of neglecting a dozen times before, which he knows she dreamed up that very moment, when she must have decided he appeared all too content and needed his equanimity disturbed.

Though no Walter Mitty or Circus McGurkus, he realizes that his circumscribed life has few, if any, opportunities, other than through dreams, of ever achieving a modicum of nobility and that reality is a "ball-buster," whose reigning queen is his wife, whom he innocently settled for on receiving his draft notice, before heading off to the Normandy beachheads to defend democracy against the Nazis, a lowly soldier toting an M-1, backpack filled with C rations, and a belt of grenades, who returned home prematurely with a Purple Heart for shrapnel wounds sustained to his groin and brain, "an impotent freak," his wife confided to her friends, whose only chance for gainful employment was at the local factory, geared up to produce ball bearings for every imaginable machine of destruction the politicians referred to as "vital industry" matériel, where he became the night watchman/maintenance man, sweeping up, with his horse-hair broom, compound he'd sprinkle on the hardwood floors of that 150,000-square-foot complex, then retracing his steps with a bucket of sudsy disinfectant to wet-mop the same area, a factory that now makes commodes, tubs, and sinks, where he has the same job for life, provided he can keep hunting green leviathans, believing he'll eventually harpoon one with his mop or broom.

A Thing for Red

Who let the trickster loose again today? There he goes, taunting the young ladies, sticking his tongue out like a serpent, trying to triangulate their erogenous zones, speak the cunnilingua franca of love, face to face with each, poking his head into everybody's business before the constabulary runs him in for venery, vagrancy, sodomy — that old goat, Biblical reprobate!

Ah, but he's a slick one, that sly dodger, who goes by so many names and disguises it's impossible, at any given moment, to locate his undulating, protean shade: there he is, behind President Bill's eyebrows; now he's hiding between Pima-cotton sheets in the Kennedy/Monroe honeymoon suite; now he's FDR's crutches, Castro's cigars, Gorbachev's birthmark, Waldheim's lie. He's the abracadabra spin doctor of cosmic politics, the universal agitator, galactic catalyst for moral turpitude.

Uh-oh! Now he's inside my trousers! Pious as an archbishop giving communion, he's appropriated my pen and penis to write himself large on this horny morning, pawning himself off as upright, over here at my corner table in this noisy restaurant, pretending to be a straight-arrow poet composing free-verse romantic fantasies, subliminal sonnets and odes to Helens and Ledas, not coveting all the women in the place, especially the red-headed hostess, who keeps winking at me. Now he's my priapic head of state; now my volcanic erection, threatening to erupt, sully the puce tablecloth cloaking my concupiscence; now he's crotch-lava, flowing down my pant legs; now my self-conscious consternation, contemplating whether to attempt an inconspicuous escape or wait for the trickster to detumesce and slither away, undetected, to see what mayhem he might yet incite by getting in the redhead's hair, under her skin.

'Twas the Day After Xmas

Xmas done come 'n gone like a fart in a worldwind, and all I got left now is left holdin' the bag (and I don't mean a dog bag brimmin' over 'n under with nauseal turkey leftovers from Redbird's turkey farm, neither), left high 'n dry on a Gulligan's island o' bills, my Master 'n Visa like two ship-wracked victims stranded nekkid on a niceberg in the Artick, left without a choice but get my ass back in gear, back into the plant, this Friday mornin', and me almost the only jerk off or on the road, since no one else in his right nor wrong minds neither would volunteer his services to do General Grunt work, inspectin' faulty wirin' harnesses 'n misinstalled hairbags, 'cause the company asked for volunteer assholes who'd give up their sleepin'-in rights on what everybody else considers a unadulteried holiday, pure 'n simple, even if he ain't doin' it outten the goodness o' his hard nor company loyalties neither but rather 'cause his old lady done spent him outten house 'n hole, buyin' herself the Xmas he didn't have no time to buy noways for bein' too damn busy boltin' down them motor mounts in the first, second, 'n third places first, 'n second 'cause he can't stand buyin' all that shit in the third place anyways. Bottom line is that ol' Saturn 69's payin' time times three, equalin' triple time, which transplants into sixty-six buckaroos a hour, which ain't turkey feed nor lint-in-your-pocket change neither, if you catch the drift o' my bank's overdraft.

Jeezus, but this goin'-back-next-day stuff sucks the You'll-tide all-day peppermint lick-stick big one! Used to be union wouldn't allow no exceptionables — you had to take day 'fore 'n aft off, like bread on a caviar sammich — but what with outsizin' 'n downsourcin' 'n all, not to mention good ol' recalls on standard human-air fuckups requirin' overtime just to get back to squares two 'n three, the UA o' W done lost all its cloud with the company. It's no damn wonder your average John Blow 'n Joanne Dough gotta look for sloppy seconds 'n suck hind tails, while Vito I-o'-ca-ca floats to earth on a golden parasail paved in gold without never bruisin' his fat-cat ass landin' on the White House lawn.

I swear to shit, it all stinks to high hell on high. The rich die richer, while the ain't-gots live forever belly-up, declarin' bankrupture, the real Charter 11 variety, without no belt-loopholes to keep 'em afloat in Florta or the Cavemans or let 'em start up again with millions in preserve in some Swiss-cheese banked account. Oh, fuck it! I'm just pissed 'cause I ain't in their Nike Mike Jordans.

Truth is, Xmas day 'n day after with the missus ain't all that swift noways — never is. Fack is, I kind o' hate all the fuss. My old lady's like a kid openin' its gifts, gigglin' 'n awin' 'n cryin' with excitements 'n joy. Thing is, she's the one does all the buyin' for me 'n herself (mostly herself), like it's supposed to be a big Santy surprise, who done left all that shit at the bottom o' the chimbly in exchange for some moldy Nillas, a bowl o' cat milk, some kittie litters, dog bones, 'n dog bags with turkey leftovers, which we still got from Redbird's Gobbler Day giveaway blowout.

Jeezus! Durin' this time o' the year, she goes totally apeshit, like her Mr. Master 'n Mrs. Visa is card blanch or buffalo chips in Wild Bison Bill's floatin' crapshoot on the Missus-Sloppy. Usually, durin' the rest o' the real year, she just spends my bread on run-o'-the-general-mills necessitaries from Wal-Fart, Tarzhay, and JC Pennay, them three French companies vyin' with the Japs to buy up the home o' the braves, if no longer the land o' the freebies. Truth is, like I said, the old lady can't help herself, come Xmas; even more truth is, I can't help myself neither, for goin' down the tubes so fast I got no choice but pick up some extra moonshinin' at sixty-six Bison Bills a hour.

So, here I am over to Fenton, to good ol' Saturn 69, only I only see one other car on the whole damn lot, which I reckelnize as Alferneeze's. (Only a uppity nig climbin' the corporal ladder like it was a palmed tree in Afurca, droopin' with Confirmative Reaction cuckoonuts just there for the grabbin' — so long's the hand doin' the grabbin's blacker'n the one-eye jack o' spades — only one o' them "Afurcan-a-Mericans" could afford one o' them fancy Izoozoo Ground Trooper Land Rover-in-the-Clover Grant Cherry-key SBD's, while the rest of us chumps gotta tool around in ten-year-olds Cutlet Supremes 'n preowned half-ton Dodge Rambler pickups.) Natch, I get suspiculous that somethin' ain't quite up to snuffs, when Alferneeze gets outten his SBD and, right off the cup, sticks his hand out to wish me a happy Xmas.

"Well, seems like we got ourselves a little problem here."

"Yeah, like what?" I says.

"Seems like none of the other guys who volunteered for inspection is showin' up today. They all called in sick."

"Sick? Don't you mean *ripped*?"

"Whatever. Problem is, we can't do no inspectin' with just the two of us."

"Well, bullshit!" I says. "I'm rarin' to work. Ain't that I need to, so much as I feel like I owe the company one for the road."

"Well, *I* sure don't," he says. "Think I'd be here if I wasn't line boss? Like to be home right now, with the kids and wife. Looks like I'm gonna get to after all."

And me seein' them sixty-six Bison Bills a hour goin' down the crapper faster'n shit hittin' a ovulatin' fan in a wind tunnel, thinkin', Jeezus, am I screwed now, 'cause I need them extra five hundred greens a whole helluva lot more than Alferneeze don't.

"Thanks for showin' up, anyway" he says. "Sorry to put you to any inconvenience."

"Not to worry. I got plenty o' plans with the wife, and she'll be damn happy to see me home."

"OK. We'll see you Monday. Merry Christmas to y'all!"

"Back at you, boss!"

So he blasts outten the lot, with me right behind him,

only now I got a big decision to make: do I head home now, goggle over all that shit the missus done got yesterday from 'n for her 'n herselfs, get laid, eat myself to death, later this aft, on her day-after-Xmas feast, or do I head over to Redbird's first, for some warmup pregame grub, then over to Fubar's, to get into some pigskin action on their herd o' big-screen TV's, tank up on Xmas spirits (a dozen or so Bud Light brewskies), 'n *then* go home, goggle over all that shit the missus done got yesterday from 'n for her 'n herselfs, get laid, 'n eat myself to death on her cream-spinach special, chuck-full o' oysters, 'n her roast beast, drizzled with her own recipe for Holland Days Bernice sauce? (Mmm-mmm, that's good eatin', guarangoddamnteeya, not to mention all the other fixin's 'n trimmin's she learned to whip up from her mom — who done learned all her fancied cookin' off the TV, breakfast, lunch, 'n dinner times, from Julius Childs, Graham Cracker O' Cur, Justice Wilson (the Gallopin' Cajun), Okra Windfree, 'n Richmond Simmons — especially that gooey pee-can pie that gets your fingers so sticky lickin' 'em's almost as good as the pie itself.)

Suddlenly, I remember what I done just said to Alferneeze about rarin' to work. What horseshit that was, not to mention me owin' the company one for the road! Truth is, company owes me one big fat one over sixty-six for the road, and I'm goin' to claim it right now, soon's I tie on a feedbag stockin' at Redbird's. Fubar's, clear your chimbley, 'cause Santy's comin' down to snatch his snacks, and I don't mean moldy Nillas, a bowl o' cat milk, some kittie litters, dog bones, 'n dog bags with turkey leftovers, if you catch the drift o' my day-after-Xmas draft beers!

The Rehabilitation
of a War Criminal

On a civil-service application, he listed his birthplace as "Hölle, Germany," his age as "ancient," marital status as "implausible." He signified his faith and race as "atheist" and "Aryan," with a strain of Teutonic consanguinity dating back to Leif the Lucky, dotting his anonymous name with swastikas. He listed his previous occupations as "Systematic Exterminator," "Sadistic Sperm Surgeon," "Stirpiculturist," "Theoretical Recolonizer of Aliens," "Obliterator of Ethics and Education." To the month and day, he was able to recall the start and finish of each phase of his work experience.

In the space reserved for **Further Remarks**, he explained why he was presently seeking employment: "I need the job, bad, to survive; will report seven days a week, Sabbath, all holidays; will stay late, stand eight hours, if required, relocate, salute the clock, inform on neighbors, spy on acquaintances — in short, perform functions others might consider demeaning. Self-abasement is a quality with which I'm more conversant than most."

On the line beneath the referrals section, **References — Recommendations**, he scrawled the terse non sequitur "Inconceivable," hoping to reassure his potential superiors that he wouldn't act out of compassion or show personal concern.

Finally, he scribbled his illegible signature, authenticating his statements as true and, to the best of his knowledge, sane.

Weeks later, from a thousand candidates, he was selected and, pledging his allegiance to the flag, assigned the rank of itinerant state arbitrator in cases of unemployment-benefits claims, medical malpractice, and racial discrimination.

Going Ape

I awaken into a wide facsimile of sleep this late-December lunes-day. Who I was last evening, before my fatigued body bedded down, left its drowsy senses to the irresponsible keeping of dreams, I don't recall at all, my former identity fettered deep within the intellect's desperate network. Even my eyes refuse to recognize the reflection peeking out at me from the bathroom mirror as they assess my naked, hirsute, simian physique — australopithecine cranium, chimpanzee limbs, hands, and toes, opposable thumbs — a grotesque primate lost in the rain forest of my dazed gaze, anachronistic, lethargic, an Old World ape whose brain has taken its anus's place, its face scrunched in time's vise, a pre-Pleistocene survivor, whose dragging scrotum somehow holds the future of my species, *Homo sapiens.*

Could this creature sizing me up know who I am despite my troubling fugue? And why has it come to this? Could I be the missing link in the chain of being that once hung from the ceiling of Heaven, or am I just suffering delusions of devolution by equating my genealogy with that of a fucking chimp? Jesus, what genetic glitch has dismantled me, caused me to question my origins, brought me to such an impasse that I loathe acknowledging my humble forebears?

Maybe I've come so far as a man, with wisdom that transcends understanding, understanding instinct, that admitting I once locomoted on all fours, swung from fifty-foot creepers, ate sweet green trees leaf by leaf by leaf, pissed and shit alfresco, fornicated in plain view of group members is too embarrassing to share with my peers and superiors, too crude to own up to, truth to the primal common denominator so absolutely pure, so unequivocally sublime, that doing so would be tantamount to conceding original sin.

Suddenly, my razor blade draws blood, staining my full-grown beard. Instead of washing it off, I let it dry, decide to apply no cologne or deodorant this morning, refuse to dress, then storm out the front door, lope down the street to the nearest tree capable of sustaining my weight, and begin tracing the vine system I'll take downtown to work.

Dreaming of Dying in the Saddle

Yippee-ki-yay-ki-yo! I'm just an ol' cowhand from the Rio Grande, who don't know his ass from a hole in his head, his balls from ostrich eggs or granny's dumplin's, his dick from a miner's pick, a switch of beef jerky, or an ugly-stick to beat off Sweet Betsy from Pike and her entourage of travelin' Clementines when they get shore leave from the good ship *Pequod*.

I don't know shit from Shinola neither, a garbanzo bean from Lydia Pinkham's little liver pills, Fillmore West from James Fillimore Cooper, Filbert the Frog, Philomena, Filliam of Orange, or Wilhelm "Al" Shake-Speer, last known bastard son of Moishe and Wilhelmina Cohen, who immigrated to Hebron from Berlin at the height of Hitler's Easter-egg Jew hunt to pursue an active role in survival.

Yippee-ki-yay-*l'chaim*, I say, whenever the going gets so tough I get saddle burns on my chin, parched-cross buns, lover's nuts so bodacious I could eat five buffaloes, hides on, for lunch and drive a thousand beeves three hundred miles, by sundown, to Jackson Hole-in-the-Wall without stoppin' to choke a chicken or pinch a loaf, just to prove I'm one heck of a tough sombitch.

I figger, some day, my Princess Di will come to save me from these lonesome nights on the plains. After all, old dogs *can* learn new tricks if they got a bitchin' mistress to teach 'em how to tell a clit from catnip, tits from Tater Tots and broccoli tips, you know, yer basic chuck-wagon grub. Truth is, too many nights on the trail take a troll's toll, make pubes sprout on yer palms!

Yippee-*chaim*-eee-ki-oooooh! Hi-yo, Rosebud, away! Gotta hit the trail again, pilgrim, make sure when I come to the fork in the road I take it, don't run away with the spoon, get knifed in my kishkes. I may not know a Kimono dragon from a Malarian tapir, but you can bet yer bottom buckaroo I ain't gonna die with my boots on in Bumblefuck, Bolivia, or without a hard-on, in bed with Etta Place, dinin' out at the Y.

Yippee-ki-K-Y-ki-oy!

In Defense of the Nation's Honor

Yesterday, aftermath of New Year's Eve, he put his overloaded mind on cruise control, took a long drive into the cerebral countryside, via a winding, heavily billboarded interstate paralleling the under-construction information superhighway, content to rely on his television set, that road most traveled by, to bring him that old tried-and-trusty-true championship college football, most of the best of it, anyway, rolled into one hypnotizing bowl of bowls: Boredom.

Yesterday, in a singular inauguration of his spirit into the Malingerer's Hall of Fame, he discovered the depths of his depravity, taking the couch potato's oath of allegiance to the country's fanatical passion, swearing on a stack of pretzels and six-pack of Bud to be honest and faithful in his duties to the people who'd elected him Chump, Chief Asshole and Bottlewasher of the Nether World, which require him to show endless devotion to the sport, keep track of standings, records broken — the whole hundred yards — every Saturday and Sunday afternoon, Monday night, or whenever the intrepid networks can shoehorn one more NutraSweet Tournament of Dandelions into a time slot for viewers willing to endure yet another N(umbing)-rated "entertainment package."

Yesterday, he achieved orgasm, satori, nirvana, surfing at least three channels eight hours straight, surfeiting his hedonism on America's sweet G spot, ready to defend his nation again, make the ultimate sacrifice, at the next New Year's Day Bay of Pigskin invasion.

Paradise Endangered

When I factor in the leading economic indicators and discover that inflation is still abating, I'm left with a nauseating twitch in the pit of my stomach, but I don't know why or what's motivating my sensitivity. Apparently, the Fed and its accessories have restructured government policy to allow for growth in the bond market. Their secret is to stimulate competition, pure and simple — ferocious, untrammeled competition.

Take, for example, the Reagan administration's deregulation of the airlines or the breakup of Ma Bell to permit Sprint, MCI, and a Pandora's box of smaller emulators, no less tenacious in their cloned promotions, to pander to us little guys. After all, it's been a bull run for sixty-two months, the longest string since George Washington, with no diminishment in view. Nowadays, Wall Street's old rules of thumb no longer hold water, unless . . . unless . . .

Hey! What am I saying? This isn't my bailiwick. I'm a literary historian, a tenured professor at an Ivy League school, well-credentialed, of course, with a healthy retirement plan, all the amenities accorded a Milton specialist like me, who, for almost forty years, has taught *Lycidas*, *Areopagitica*, "When I Consider . . . ," both *Paradise*s, as well as my fair share of Freshman Comp and the *Norton Anthology* version of literary apotheosis.

What the hell do I know about supply-side and trickle-down economics, the rhetoric of big bucks, other than what I pick up, by osmosis, from CNN's *Moneyline News Hour*, *USA Today*'s financial section, and PBS's *Nightly Business Report*, that trinal wellspring of conventional wisdom, spewing and spouting, as regularly as Old Faithful, how the dollar is doing against the yen, how the Dow, NASDAQ, and the S&P are performing daily, hourly, to the minute, nano- and zeptosecond? What do I know about leading economic indicators, other than that in five years I intend to retire, and I'm frightened as hell, thinking how good ol' Columbia wants to buy me out today, replace me with part-timers or T.A.'s? How will I live on Milton-shekels in Manhattan or, west of Eden, in the Jersey suburbs, where, for the last three and a half decades, I've raised my family and thrived, albeit in modest splendor?

All I can hope for in my "golden years" is that an estate planner or money manager will parse the scanty measures of my blank verse and suggest a feasible reason or rhyme as to how my wife, her pet snake, and I might climb under the money tree and, for the rest of our days, with wandering steps and slow, deconstruct "Of man's first disobedience . . . ," luxuriate in innocent ignorance, and revel in our figless nudity without guilt or shame.

The Men's Sodality Convenes at Redbird's

Just five of 'em this mornin', 'stead o' the usual seven or eight hooligans overcrowdin' that four-top like piglets sucklin' at its mama's tits, but I could already see they was overwound up to beat the bands to a pulp, tighter'n one o' them busted crank pornographs with a outside horn. They was spittin' serious static, not one o' them mackerel snappers (they're Cathlicks, swear to God on stacked Bibles; I've heard 'em too many mornin's hailin' Mary, the waitress, beggin' her to listen to their confessionals, braggin' on their kids' edjewcations at a baker's-dozen-'n-one o' the city's pinnochial schools, like St. Adolphins or Josephus o' the Bleedin' Velveeta or Sister Cheetah Riviera o' the Innocent Wino Society in Jesus) at all certain o' the slippery glacier they done got out onto, paintin' theirselfs into a real em-bare-assin' corner for a change (usually, they stick to their bailinwire, the Cathlick scene — you know, from Pope Pile to Cardinal Burnt Sourdine 'n all them sex scandals among the priesthoods — that homo business; I gotta hand it to 'em: at least they can dish the dirt) — the confab heatin' up by the second.

"Say, which one of those guys is the Jew, anyway?"

"I think it's that ugly bastard, the one with the nasty beard and picnic-tablecloth headgear, who looks like he hasn't taken a Turkish bath since his first birthday baptism."

"Jesus, Sid! His name's Arafat."

"Yeah, that's his name, though it sounds more Chinese or Jap to me."

"Wait a second, boys. He's the leader of the PLO."

"The who? What's that mean?"

"The Palestinian Liberation Organization, Sid."

"Yeah, then what's the sheeny's name?"

"Howard, the man's name is Nathan Yahoo . . . the Jew, I mean."

"Nice try, Sid. It's Netanyahu."

"Him and Clinton are peas in the same pod. Neither can win for losing face. Geez, I'd hate to have to live in their Florsheims."

"Well, I hate to kick a dead cow in the mouth, but I can't get over how filthy looking Yassir Arafat is. Can you imagine the Pope going to Rwanda, holding an audience with the Hutus and the Tutsis, dressed like a goddamn ragamahooly man, a frigging disreputable, common, homeless wino street bum and hoping to convert the heathens? Not!"

"Whoa, Sid! Rein those camels in, big guy! Redbird's isn't the desert — it's an oasis!"

"Boys, all I can say is that it's one hell of a mess over there. Be glad, by Jesus, we've got it so good here in America, even if the President is up to his hips in alligators, what with Gennifer Flowers and Paula Jones threatening to huff and puff and *blow* his house down. He's true grits."

"Yeah, you've got to hand it to him — he's got serious nads."

About that time, two o' them cronies excuses theirselfs, then two more, leavin' the one guy by hisself, apparently miffed for havin' got stuck with the tab. And maybe "miffed" ain't the right pronoun for it. Appears the longer he sits, the more miffed he gets, until miffed turns into visually pissed right before my eyes, all eyes in the place, and he commences to throwin' a major tantrum, flingin' a leftover sausage link acrost the table, like a turd in a slingshot, prob'ly more for show than contents.

Whatever, I see him headin' to the register to pay, and as he passes my booth, I hear him mumblin' somethin' that sounds like "Goddamn A-rabs and Jews! Too bad Jesus didn't die for them, too. Sure could've saved a lot of wasted taxpayers' dollars."

The Walking Dead

By nature, predilection, and training, he's a somnambulist with a touch of the poetic, who infects wakeful psyches and relies on his sardonic wit and sarcastic barbs to get him off the hook whenever his sharp tongue lands him in sticky situations with fellow-traveler phantasms, incubi, and poltergeists who spend their eons infiltrating Homo sapiens, trying to make them "come a cropper," "come atumble," expressions he acquired during his sojourn in confederated Mississippi, Tennessee, Arkansas, Alabama, and Georgia, circa 1950–2050, when he was assigned to foment unrest among the populace, ignite flash fires among blacks and whites over issues as innocuous as civil liberties and human rights, ordered to record the progress of dystopia in Memphis, West Helena, Oxford, Selma, and Forsyth County, report back to his jackbooted immediate superior, Reichsfeldmarschall Beelzebub, at whose feet he kneeled in those inchoate days of evil and chaos when making his assessments, delivering his oracles, his oneirophilosophical predictions on mankind's future, debating apocalyptic variations on the Final Solution he, now Supreme Potentate of the Netherish States, first proposed so many millenniums ago for the pestiferous primate crew of pariahs infesting terrestrial ghettos and suburbs that he almost can't recall his original Satanic whispers in the gullible ears of Paleolithic cave dwellers, Visigoths, Vandals, and Huns, theologians in the mode of Martin Luther and Savonarola, Hitlerian devotees of "beneficial genocide," almost has no need to reprise those apprentice years, for the successes he's effected in the forms of depredations, scourges, pestilent extirpations, measures taken to purge Earth of dangerous overpopulation, ensure domestic tranquillity, the moral, mental, physical, and spiritual health of mankind.

This evening, he rises from his bed of smoldering ashes, refuses to dress in cassock, surplices, and ermines, rejects miter, scepter, and censer, in order to go naked through his sweltering kingdom, keep as cool as possible traipsing through its asphyxiating vapors, while on his worldwide tour, whose theme this century — "Did You Ever Dance with the Devil by the Pale Moonlight?" — he hopes will bring fifty million new sheep into the fold. Before leaving, for reasons of protocol more than vanity, he manicures his horns, tail, and predatory toenails, knowing that in this hellacious business of disturbing the peace, stirring up the dust, he must put his best foot forward, in the anus, up the butt, to the gut of the weakest link in the Great Chain of Being, if he expects to sustain in man disaffection for and insurrection toward the common enemy: God.

Warehouse of Mannequins

In various dark areas of the warehouse, filled to its rusty, dust-breathing gills with office equipment, furnishings, and displays from defunct companies, exist graveyards exposed to all who rummage its five floors for bargains among others' ill-fated cargo.

In these makeshift cemeteries, developed over time as loads arrived unannounced and got dumped wherever a few cubic feet could be forced to absorb more debris, repose bodies and limbs in suspended animation. Dead, in a sense, yet undecayed, these corpses form a chorus of incomplete voices, a prism of missing hues, in their haphazard assemblage, piled in disquieting riot, as if a tornado had sucked an entire town inside out.

Maimed anatomies — bloodless amputations, cracks, mismatched pigments where hands, heads, and feet were switched in previous incarnations, hairless groins devoid of vaginas or penises, breasts without nipples, unseparated buttocks — belong to the anonymous occupants of these unacknowledged burial grounds, who, without being consulted, became the subjects of euthanasia experiments, before being relegated to Bergen-Belsen–like trenches. They lie in mute, amorphous confusion, like newly hatched snakes, waiting for neither death nor reassignment, although many will return from beyond the grave and be sent out to pose as useful citizens in the state's exchange pogrom-program, instituted years ago in place of abstractions like the transmigration of souls.

Yet no one from these zones of clones has ever raised a complaint; no protestations against stirpiculture, white slavery, genocide, or gang rape by psychopaths. The warehouse management is proud of its reputation for promoting equal opportunities regardless of race, age, and gender. The directors consider their calling indispensable to the continuation of regulated supply and demand in the Land of Mannequins, threatened by overpopulation and/or extinction.

Boomlay, Boom

He listens to the morning news, chooses which issues
and facts to assimilate, which to relegate to forgetting's recy-
cling bin, somewhere deep in the base of his hippocampus —
he's not really certain, nor does it matter, since the sound
bites he retains aren't qualitatively different from what gets
jettisoned.

For instance, because he likes the lyricism, the round,
snug fit of the three names at the core of the conflict being
reported this morning — Burundi, Rwanda, Uganda — he
knows he'll be repeating them all day in myriad permutations: Burundi, Rwanda, Uganda; Rwanda, Uganda, Burundi;
Uganda, Rwanda, Burundi; Rwanda, Uganda, Bugandi; Rwunda,
Burgwandi, Gruganda; with an occasional Zaire thrown in
for good measure, just to keep all the players honest, as it
were, even pious American politicians and biased ambas-
sadors, touting democracy, honest elections, peace, espous-
ing an end to insurrectionist, dictatorial regimes succeeding
each other with bestial predictability, and even the quasi-
interested French, who actually have a few thousand citizens
being threatened, not just millions of dispensable native
black bodies — Hutus, Tutsis, Voodoos in tutus, Hindus, Hot-
tentots, Hot-to-Trots, Tater Tots, Hoo-Doos, and Two-Twos
— dying like internecine flies.

By the time he arrives at his office, the litany, a monstrous
mantra, has possessed his thoughts. Instead of thinking
"infrastructure," "greenhouse gases," "Albania," "NATO," "Chinese campaign contributions," "reconstructive quadriceps-
tendon surgery," he's worked himself up into an animated
chant redolent of Vachel Lindsay, singing himself into a
somnambulistic trance that lets him pass the black security
guard without so much as a familiar nod, indeed, with a bit
of suspicion, and buoys him all the way to his cubicled work
station, where he situates himself without delay, boots up

his computer, accesses his word processor, and begins key-
ing in, with rhythmic fervor,

> *Mumbo-Jumbo, God of the Congo,*
> *Mumbo-Jumbo will hoo-doo you,*
> *Boomlay, boomlay, boomlay, boom,*
> *Congo, bongo, boomlay, boom,*

resurrecting from verses he may have read fifty years ago, in
grade school, the closest thing to an understanding of Africa
he's ever achieved, and even then, it — whatever it was he
was fed — was already obsolete, stereotypical minstrelsy . . .

> *Fat black bucks in a wine-barrel room,*
> *Beat an empty barrel with the handle of a broom,*
> *Boom, boom, boom,*
> *A roaring, epic, rag-time tune*
> *From the mouth of the Congo*
> *To the Mountains of the Moon,*
> *Boom, steal the pygmies,*
> *Boom, kill the Arabs,*
> *Boom, kill the white men, hoo, hoo, hoo . . .*

a rumbling, thumping pounding in his stomach, pounding
across his forehead, pounding down his vertebrae and legs,
until he just wants the global village to disappear, go up in
one colossal mushroom cloud and dissolve into sputtering
silence, leaving him to grope hand to mouth in a desolate
land on the planet of the apes or, better yet, an uninhabited
core floating in space, he just one more mindless microbe or
spore hurtling toward unicellular birth fifty million years
hence . . .

> *Boomlay, boomlay, boomlay, BOOM.*

Harry Carpin, Deliveryman

What a shit-eatin', sleet-freezin' mornin', not fit for man or anphibious beast like me, just one semiquatic son-of-a-bitch who makes his livelihood deliverin' seafood to restaurants and grocery stores, sunup to dusk, unless, that is, the streets get so fuckin' slick it's impossible to navigate my eighteen-wheeler in and outta loadin' docks, in which case, like today, I say, "Fuck it," return to the warehouse, deep-six my rig, and vent my intention to call it quits till conditions massively improve.

"After all," I tell my boss, "I'll be damned if I'm gonna risk my life and Fin-Co's profits on the possibility o' jack-knifin', just to dump my cargo o' fake Jap crabmeat, tainted salmon-ella, endangered doll-fin and poor-piss, 'live' African rock Maine lobster from Far Rockaway, not to mention less exotic 'catch o' the day,' like orange rugby, a-baloney, maui-wowie, monkey fish, groupie-jewfish, yellow-bellied tuna, and God only knows what other sea monsters, includin' sperm-killer whales like the one that swallowed that Bible guy and puked him up outta pure disgust onto some god-forstricken shore.

"Hey! Let's face it, I don't owe Jonas squat, even if the guy did beat God's odds — besides, I'll be back on my route tomorrow with no one the less wiser for gettin' his 'fresh' frozen fish one day late."

Back to Normal

He couldn't fathom just what was happening when it all began, the metamorphosing of ordinary reality. Quite simply, he couldn't imagine what physical mutation or act of God could cause stars to appear in place of spots on the coats of Dalmatians and leopards that scurried across his nocturnal dream-screens or make baby manta rays cling, as though they belonged, to the piebald hides of giraffes and cows. He'd never seen frogs mate with dogs, snakes with cicadas and condors, by means of their salacious, elongated tongues.

People, also, assumed strange manifestations: scarecrows, Gorgons, ghosts, numinous hobos, as well as cryptic, eerie aliens sporting three amorphous heads, reproductive organs projected through laser beams emanating from sockets hidden in their mouths.

Even bowls of cereal, plates of eggs, mashed potatoes, steak and fish and chicken, rearranged their matter before his reeling eyes, invited him to feasts fit for Pygmy dignitaries: baked-Alaska sheep skulls, octopuses in scorpion's ink, walrus-penis thermidor, spider eggs *en papillote*, and, instead of wine, venom of cobra, pit viper, blood of sperm whale, served in perspiring Grails.

Throughout his self-rearranging derangements, assailed by topsy-turvy tergiversations, he became consumed with questioning his own humanity. His sanity hung in the balance. He began to doubt mightily, on sliding into bed, that he'd ever emerge from his nightmare. Like an ostrich, he'd bury his head in solitude, hoping to elude the demons by maneuvering blindly through silence's catacombs. But nothing he might consciously orchestrate could eradicate, let alone mitigate, these visitations.

Then, one day, he awakened into a wide whiteness not unlike Alzheimer's or immortality. Everything everywhere was back to normal.

Shall Rise Again

All across this broad land, the call has gone out to Branch Davidian–like compounds, klaverns, regiments, militias, and cells of unaffiliated terrorists to confederate, take up cudgels against the Zionist conspiracy in government, the black abasement of America's pure white race. An infectious hysteria chills the shrill air, blisters and buckles the country's infrastructure. In subterranean laboratories of self-anointed Dr. Caligaris, revolution bubbles over beaker lips, replicates itself in petri dishes, whose constituents will eradicate the viruses responsible for mankind's degradation. Whatever means are necessary, these devotees will sacrifice their lives for the cause, leaving no stone unturned in their Luther-like scourge.

Rarely do these heroes of the neo-Aryan nation surface, let themselves get caught in acts of mass destruction, covert recruitment, sabotage, coercion, infiltration, weapon stockpiling. Usually, they keep a low profile, working as insidiously as moles. But yesterday, five members of a group from Pennsylvania, dedicated to the extermination of Jews holding public office, were captured robbing a bank in Morton, Illinois, attempting to ensure the solvency of their holy mission. One guy, bare toes painted Day-Glo orange, dressed in a Richard Nixon mask and Christmas-tree lights, a second, outfitted as Santa, and the others, his elfish helpers, were tripped up in their own devilment when one of their pipe bombs exploded prematurely — grains of sand blown away in an hourglass draining a desert.

Regnum Christi

This was one for the books. You ain't gonna believe it, my dad-blamed luck. Here I come into Redbird's with Excedral headsnake number sixty-nine for havin' overdid my tipplin' the night before at Fubar's, and all I'm wantin' to do is hide in a booth by myself, outten the mainstreams o' tables. But the place looked like a whale migration off Sand Francisco Cove, it was so congestated: arms was fins 'n flippers, bodies was flukes, mouths was spouts spewin' smoke 'n chatter.

Anyways, wouldn't you know it'd be my bum luck to have one o' them mackerel snappers over to the Cathlick table — the Sodality Society in the Res-erection 'n Deportation o' Jesus — the loud bastard with the unnoxious laugh that sounds like a female coyote at the height of a climax or a owlpine mountain climber yodelin' for all he's worth — Yo-do-lo-he-hay! Yo-do-lo-who-laid-the-la-dy-who? — to let someone know he's stuck under a anvilanche . . . just my fuckin' luck, with my head poundin' like a mother Lake Superior, to have that guy wattle over to the booth next to mine, right in earshots to both ears, and of all things, he's escortin' two o' them guys all in black from toe to lips 'cept for that white ring-around-the-collar thing they wear to extinguish 'em from other walkin' deads, if you catch my drift, and I'm gettin' nervouser by the second, 'cause already I know there goes my serenitude for the mornin', 'cause I can see this loud bastard is shot with the program, his inflated chest stuck out farther than his fat gut, like as if to show his cronies he's a hot shit.

As I listen to their bluster (I can't *not* listen, if you catch my wind's drift), him scrunched in between them two, with his red suspendibles about to bust their clips, his neck oozin' over his top button like overstuffed sausage poppin' outten its casin's, his bald head givin' off sweat like a flashed flood,

I begin to see he's just that: a real hot shit who don't know jack shit from Shinola! It don't take me long to finger out he fingers he's been selected or chose hisself to do the church's dirty-work biddin', act as a board o' one to choose a new ministerial o' the Lord, priest or whatnot, to lead their herd o' sheeps.

So he starts in, interviewin' these two zombies (who, as I axledently easedrop too far over, I learn just flew in from a sementary in Hobroken), askin' the dumbest questions I ever heard, so profoundly ignint I can't sit in peace, gather strengths to take on Friday mornin' by the bullhorns, get my shit together to hit my shift with somethin' approximatin' pissin' vigor, me havin' to listen to the bastard conduck a Hispanic Imposition, consistin' of absolutely nil about popes, archbishopricks, sementarians, priests, archdiseases, whoredinations, High Masts, babtismals, cat-o'-jisms, the difference between Jismwits 'n some order I missed for his jerksome laughter — the nervous kind, you know, that grows like crab grass up through your zoysia.

But all of a suddlenly, they turn the tables over on him, start up their own imposition.

"John, what do you know about Regnum Christi?"

"Regnum Christi?" he asks, shakin' his purpleplexed head. "What's that?"

"It's what our order contributes to the church," one o' them deads speaks. "It means 'Kingdom of Christ.' We try to enlist good souls like you from the laity to serve as gobetweens — intercessors, if you will — between the mother church and her blessed children."

"How's that translate bottom line, in layman's terms?"

I can almost hear him beginnin' to squirm acrost from me, worried shitless, now, that somehow he done got hisself over his head in a barrel o' quicksand.

"Well, John, we'd like to induct you into Regnum Christi, the first of your congregation to be so honored, make you a Missionary in Jesus."

He don't know what to say — I can tell by the pregnant pausality that produces at least five baby hippos 'n two elephumps before he can regain his decomposure.

"Jesus!" he splutters. "I don't know what to say. You two've really got me caught over a barrel!"

"Just say yes, and we'll take the rest from there."

"Well . . . well . . . I'm not sure I'm your best guy, if you know what I mean."

"'Jonathan 'John' McNamara, Regnum Christi.' Sounds mighty good to us," both deads chime in to onced.

"Well . . . well . . . ," I hear him stutterin', flustered as all hell, who prob'ly begun wonderin' how he done mired hisself so deep in his own papal bull.

So I stay just long enough to watch him slunk to the register, with the two death-warmed-overs followin' behind, all stately 'n spit-shined 'n lookin' like a couple o' boardin'-school fagnits, and his cronies at the table he regularly sits at gigglin', guffawin', snickerin', I'm thinkin', though I can't tell for sure for their bein' evasional, hidin' behind wide-open newspapers so's not to be seen, the ostrick thing people do when they wanna be insuspiculous. And I see him, this McNamara guy, ease outten the door, still too damn numb 'n dumb to feel the freight train that done just run him over like a ton o' bricks, with his two shadows in tow.

Then I get up myself to go, past the Fattycan Council of Archbishopricks' table, just as one o' them guys is crackin' up, a smart-ass wise-guy type, who's apparently got some info, insider info at that, unconventional wisdom, which I overhear in passin' out.

"John's really fixed his broken plumbing now, for damn sure! Those guys he's with, they're the strong-arm body of the Church, and they've got him by the Fig Newtons, alright! I should know. I'm the one who called Archbishop McGee and told him John'd be good for a big hit, since he's been bragging all month about getting that big highway construction bid. What John doesn't know is that he just said

Ave Maria to five green grand to become an honorary ass-hole of the lay brigade!"

Steppin' into the bracin' Friday smog, I could see my headsnake had done wriggled off into the undergrass, and all I kept thinkin', drivin' all the way to work, was thank God there's enough chumps in the world to save us undis-believers from bein' too conspiculous in God's eyes.

A Small Investor

Having just endured the business report on his car radio, he tries to size up the worldwide economy in one fell swoop of his breakfast-bound imagination but readily realizes his expertise is severely limited, especially since he once believed that the Dow was a military-industrial-complex company infamous for producing napalm, which America's troops used on the gooks in Vietnam, and Agent Orange, which they sprayed to defoliate their family trees; once believed "NASDAQ" was an abbreviation similar to "Nazi," adopted by Hitler's inner circle in the late '20s; believed the term "prime" was the finest cut from a loin of beef or referred to the *first* person born on earth (Adam or Eve up for grabs then, despite the literalness of the rib business in Genesis, since he doubted a man could ever have a baby).

With invidiousness he inherited from his father (who was tortured for three years during World War II, in a cave on Saipan, having both testicles crushed, one hand and both ears hacked off, his brains so scrambled that when he came home, he holed up in his basement and never surfaced again, except to be transferred, via the embalmer, to his final grave), he equates the Nikkei with a vast, red rising sun, symbolic of samurai domination of the West; suffers paranoia so strangling that in nightmares he feels invasions of bats, infestations of rats crawling all over his sleeping body, gnawing, eating his balls, his fingernails, his mind, each of the millions of insidious creatures, squeaking and screeching, wearing the face of either Tojo or Hirohito himself; refuses to drive a Jap car, watch a Jap TV, click a Jap camera, call home on a Jap cell phone, eat anything resembling sushi.

He believed, until a few years ago, that stocks and bonds were whips and chains, a code phrase, perhaps, for sado-masochistic stuff perpetrated on working stiffs by an international consortium of greedy Jews indulging in collusive tactics through a cartel funneling laundered currency into offshore mutual funds, futures and options on pork bellies and lean hogs, high-tech companies and utilities to ensure they'd get back all the money, paintings, and real-estate holdings, if not the multitude of human lives, stolen from them during the Holocaust.

If only he knew a bit more about how the economy works, he might share in America's apparent wealth, described in confusing detail on the evening news as 6122, 6650, something about bulls routing bears, a new record high every night, something to do with five-hundred-million-plus shares changing hands daily out of a single exchange on Wall Street. But all he knows is that he's in hock up to his boxers, just trying to make mortgage and car payments, provide food and clothes for his wife, two kids, and himself, not to mention keep up with union dues, taxes, tithes at Most Precious Blood, insurance a luxury he couldn't afford if it weren't for the Allstate branch at Piggly Wiggly. If only he'd been born different, born rich, born with a gold spoon between his lips, who's to say what he'd be doing right this minute instead of eating breakfast at a dumpy diner at 4:48 in the a.m., trying to get himself ready to clock in to butcher this morning's five sides of beef?

"Bullshit! Horseshit! Pigshit!" he snorts; then, recognizing where, who, he is, he shifts on a dime, comes to his senses again, knowing, as he's always known, that he can weather corrections, inflation, recessions just by continuing to invest in himself, the best stock of all, never selling short or taking profits early, rather holding on for the long haul.

The Vanity of Human Delusions

All our privileged lives, we pressure ourselves to get ahead, burn the candle from the middle outward, to both ends, along an invisible wick, teach ourselves to lie down with fleas so we can wake up with dog-dreams to keep the demons at bay. We choose our soul mates but not until they've been reduced on final markdown, despite history's no-return policy. We go about advertising ourselves like frenetic advance men tacking circus posters to telephone poles or Burma Shave placards to tomato stakes in antic succession at the edges of cornfields mapping a nation's byways. We die a thousand deaths in a single breath when asked, by unanimous consent, at the Convention of Universal Ambulance Chasers to run for assistant editor to the chief speechwriter for all impeached presidents, the honor, acclaim, potential riches to be derived from sacrificing ourselves to public service all overwhelmingly compelling. We take the Fifth as a matter of course during the throes of our deathbed confessions, to avoid incriminating ourselves and losing our souls. After all, regardless of our vast education, we never seem to grasp the implications of election and grace, rarely realize in time that the candle's flame sputters, no matter where it flickers, in the absence of inspiration, dogcatchers only catch fleas when they go to bed sweaty in the rice paddies of their dreams, 180 degrees southwest of East Jesus, and that neither Adam nor Eve were big bargains to generations of begats who inherited their hand-me-down pratfalls.

So where does all this leave me, leave us, who're left shoveling into Glad Bags clods of elephant shit steaming along the parade route long after the Greatest Show on Earth has repackaged itself into the latest chautauqua incarnation in Chicago or San Diego to entertain the body politic with the newest magical elixirs for the human spirit? Should we strike, demand better treatment for inmates, better wages, sanitary conditions, pensions, better Medicare provisions for old age, or should we stay, raise the ante, and call, hoping our bluff will be persuasive enough to convince Satan to fold, play with himself under the table, throw in his cards, cash in his ill-gotten chips, get the hell out of town, join up with the circus somewhere beyond Telluride, where he can sign on as a clown, earn his putty nose and honk-horn, become leader of the dung brigade, go to sleep with flea bites itching, and wake up with elephantiasis?

Ah, sweet dreams, sweet Prince. Parting is such sweet sorrow. *Hasta la vista!* Until the morrow! *Adiós!* Either we'll see ya or we won't!

My Life as an Egg Beater

The human organism is a very complex scheme. I take this truism on faith, take it to mean that the sky's the limit when eating's at stake: binging, starving, and everything in between, thirsting, drinking to satiety, getting inebriated when all else fails. Otherwise, how could I, when I'm not even hungry, possibly order Egg Beaters with mushrooms — no potatoes or even garnish on the plate — dry toast with "lite" margarine on the side, and decaf coffee, knowing that each is loaded, teeming with tasteless or artificially flavored, colorless or dyed toxins, hidden, insidious chemicals, contaminants, death particles disguised as natural ingredients, low-/no-fat, low-/no-cholesterol agents tamed, like isotopes, to yield societal benefits, make life easier to manage, promote vigor in laboratory rats, keep the corporate and cultural waistlines svelte or at least not oozing over the belt?

The human organism is a miracle, synecdoche for ecosystem, global village, galaxy, a victory garden, unassailed in its diversity. How incredible that certain of the species *Homo sapiens* can smoke cigarettes — crave nicotine, tars, inhale carcinogens as they would pure oxygen — and not asphyxiate themselves, destroy their lips, gums, lungs, and nails. Oh, and other substance abuse — tranquilizers, opiates, vitamins, pain relievers that alter our minds and bodies — our national pastime: addiction.

Naturally, I have good days and bad, moments when I think I see through all this, penetrate to the truth's absolute — that each human being is living proof that existence isn't an aberration but a Rube Goldberg gizmo, a DNA locomotive out of control, a spaceship to Uranus two quarts low — and Prozac moments when I don't give a shit.

Chronic Absenteeism

On his way to work, this dank, gray Monday, he drives past dreary houses surrounded by dormant grass, melting snow, their splotchy plots snot-filled handkerchiefs or ghettos leveled to flush the last Jew from hiding, from his undependable memory of times leached into forgetting over half a century, from existence in a world gone insane.

Suddenly, he spies a shapeless black lump that could be any animal's carcass were it not for the synaptic flash that lets him register this anomaly as a frozen crow, splayed on its back, eyes heavenward in an attitude of arrogant outrage. His shock is a plastic bag thrust over his head. He gasps; breathing seizes, ceases. The past goes out and in and out of focus. He's never seen one of these scavenging creatures dead, never had any reason to hope that someday the species might vanish from the planet.

As he reaches the four-way stop, recovers in time to punch his brakes to the floor, he encounters a *Korps* of crows strutting back and forth from shoulder to median, oblivious of rush-hour traffic, carrying off beakfuls of hapless possum — fur, skin, sinew, organs, bones. All the way to his office, he shudders, cringes, then arrives to begin another missed day.

Planet of the Prime Apes

The café bristles, this chilly, wet Wednesday, with conversation by apes of all varieties, though chimpanzees predominate. They're huddled in family bands around the room, table after circular table, chittering, barking, grunting animatedly, gesturing wildly with arms and legs, their fingers and lips stippling the air, frowning, smiling, scowling, expressing outrage, disbelief feigned and genuine, laughing boisterously, their voices more screeches than articulations, one group discussing O.J.'s economic Armageddon, another the state of the Catholic Church today contrasted with its glorious past, a third, consisting of six high-school kids who could be terrorists or hackers in the making, sporting shaved heads or bowl cuts, rampant acne, Coke-bottle glasses with tortoiseshell frames, talking about their heroes — Hitler, Pantera, Quentin Tarantino, Bill Gates — and take-home essays "up the butt" instead of exams (the world is their PC oyster in a laptop nutshell); a fourth miniconfederation convened over breakfast, dressed to the nines, confine their strident palaver to the Dow and S&P 500 — the stock market's Klondike and Sutter's Mill over the last five years, that insatiable feeding frenzy of bulls and golden calves alike.

The room crackles with spirited rataplan as though it were a zoo or rain forest, not a local café halfway between Hades and Darth Vader's Empire. Meanwhile, I keep to myself in this remote booth, a lay sociologist or anthropologist taking notes on their strange intercourse, these garrulous chimps so human in their socialization one might easily attribute to them more sophisticated and subtle design, more elevated mentality, than their simian intellects demonstrate. I sit by myself, shivering with fear that, at any moment, the whole volatile place will reach flash point, explode in flames, I a lonely lowland silverback cut loose from my family so many millenniums ago I don't even remember when the rift occurred, a wandering primate who yet locomotes quadrupedally, is yet a vegetarian, and yet wears a hirsute robe about my massive frame, cloaked head to toe in my own stench, my only redeeming feature my invisibility. Ah, yes, I've perfected the high art of camouflage, keeping out of sight despite my size, protecting my privacy from all manner of beasts.

After all, if these loquacious apes could see me writing, they'd stone me, roast my skin to a crisp on a spit, and, after feasting on my savory meat, a singular delicacy, pulverize my charred bones, mix the remaining grit into wafers or with medieval opiates and nostrums to make sweet, sacred wine they'd consume in eucharistic ecstasy approximating blessed orgasm, obliterating, unwittingly, the last link to their primordial instincts for tolerance, friendship, and love.

Death's Bridegroom

Early each morning, waking is an act of beatific contrition, of inordinate humbling, as he stumbles from rumpled sheets into the frigidity of the electricityless room, naked, shivering, disoriented, groping, like Oedipus and Beethoven and van Gogh in their later stages of entropy, through a blind, deaf, dissociated fugue so bright, so amplified, so coherent and reasonable, so logical and emblematic of prudent free will, no one unaware of his affliction would ever guess his essence has been losing ground for at least three decades, ever since that tryst when death, disguised as love, first beguiled him with its bisexual wiles, deceived him into believing that trust and respect were inviolable and that matrimony, like a medieval talisman, could ward off internecine purges, plagues, virulent pandemics, even genocides, at least thirty years since he genuflected to love in the name of freedom and spontaneity, a score and ten or more since he and love first conceived the possibility of children, fusing their genetic energy to perform magic, procreate the entire race of Homo sapiens in one generative copulation, one mindless ejaculation, he vomiting both semen and egg in random abandon, until nine months from then and there, the descendants of Satan ascended out of their nether cave and blessed them, such an odd couple, with a raison d'être, an excuse for perpetuating those marriage vows they made in youthful haste, commingling their spirits "forever." . . .

No one who wasn't a close friend before marital discord transformed him into a vicious satyr given to orgiastic grotesqueries, self-destructive demonstrations of the most monstrous kind, would ever believe how docile and sensitive this Quasimodo had been before losing his way, dropping from hope's womb into a world of disillusion, when he sold his soul to death for sex, not even for gratification so much as the fulfillment of some vague, dormant fantasy, that he might prove to the universe he was a man capable of creating life from his life, needing neither a woman's fertile loins nor a Thanatotic succubus.

This wintry dawn, so forlorn and premonitory, he fumbles for his trifocals and falls to the floor, gashing his forehead on the metal bedpost. Unconscious for eons, he swims up his bleeding stream to oneiric Thebes, Bonn, Arles, upon whose preternatural shores he lies naked for a morning that stretches the length of tomorrow, before awakening again into his beatific, contritional self and recognizing he's home, in Pandemonium.

All Greeks to Me

"**D**id you hear the Greeks just discovered a new use for sheep? Wool!"

He guffaws like a kid who done farted in class, and the rest o' the table takes a laughin' jag like a convoy o' quails flushed outten the brush by a bear.

"I used that one on my secretary — name's Plopalodapolous."

"Sounds like a Loch Ness monster!"

"No, she's Greek as the ace of spades — don't ask me to spell her."

"You know what elephants use for tampons?" another says.

"Corn dogs on a stick?" one of 'em intersects.

"No! Sheep!"

On that one, the whole group lets out a giganic Brinks cheer.

"Hear the one about the Chinese guy who was buying up all the yens he could get his mitts on, then selling them to a bank in Los Angeles? He buys low, sells high. Does this four or five times."

"Where does he get the yens from?"

"How the fuck should I know, Sid? It doesn't make any difference! You're screwing up the joke!"

"OK! OK!"

"Go ahead," all of 'em beg the one on stage.

"Anyway, he comes into the bank with a wad of yens, wanting to sell them for greenbacks up the wazoo. Lady teller gives him a real low rate of exchange this time. He squeals like a stuck pig. She says, 'Sorry. It's the fluctuations.' He says, 'What?' She says, 'So sorry, but it's the fluctuations.'"

All the while, this guy's tryin' to do a Chinese accent for the Chink.

"'Fruckyouasians? What mean these fruckyouasians?' the Chink asks. 'It's the fluctuations, mister. Take it or leave it.'

'Burrshit!' he yells. 'Fruck you Amelicans, too!'"

The table explodes like someone done tied piped bombs to their feet.

"You boys see the beautiful sunrise this morning? It was the color of your shirt," one guy says, pointin' to another's arid-escent red sweater with patches.

"Yeah, what's it the sailors say? 'Red sun in the morning...'"

"Yeah, 'red sun in the morning, storm warning coming soon,' or some such. Can't remember."

"Didn't Jesus say something about what you can't see don't worry about anyway or something? Said it to the arrogant Pharisees."

"Anyway, was one hell of a sunrise, whatever it means."

"Doesn't mean shit to me, boys, if it doesn't melt the ice today."

"Hear about the Greeks?" a guy who just arrived says, tryin' to catch hisself right up to speeds. "They just discovered a new use for sheep: wool!"

The table don't raise a eyelash. Silence settles like rotten apples fallin' off a dead tree or radiators from an antomic bomb over Nagasuki.

"A new use for sheep: wool!" he repeats to another seated unovation.

"Yeah, and I heard they invented three kinds of columns, too: Caribbean, dork, and ironic!"

"Yeah, and I heard that in the Olympic Games, the Greeks ran telethons, jumped naked, threw up the biscuits, and hurled the java!"

"I heard that the winner of those games got a coral wreath!"

"Ever hear of Socrates? He was a former Greek teacher."

"Wasn't he a philosopher?"

"That, too, Sid. Jesus! He died from an overdose of wedlock."

"And they were all eventually conquered by the Romantics, right?"

"No, Howard, by their sheep, who learned how to shear them and use their hemlocks for pillow ticking and quilt down."

"Jesus, Sid! Cool it! What gives with that shit?"

At that point, I look over to my right and see a whole family o' Chinks or Philipagans or Sam Owens, you know, the ones with the black hair that shines like someone done dipped it in a vat o' granola oil, skin plastered with banana peels, and them eyes that could be pimpkin seeds — slanty — and I'm thinkin' how maybe they heard the Chink joke and now they got hurt feelin's, the six of 'em, kids 'n all. They got as much rights to eat here at Redbird's as us, even if some of us got our manners up our butts. Sometimes I feel like tellin' them loudmouth Pope Pile Twenty-thirds they don't own the whole damn place, just one table, but then I always believe in live 'n let live on, if you catch my drift.

And truth is, I like a good Greeks or Polack or Jew or Jap or Chink joke myself when it's real clever 'n gut-bustin'ly funny, no matter it cuts across all ethnicalities, threatenin' to em-bare-ass one race at the expenditure of another. I mean, come the hell on! That holier-than-now stuff gets real tired. We're all of us Armanians 'n kikes sometimes. I mean, we all do stupid things, stick our foots in the bucket, our tits in the ringer, our dicks in a vice grip every onced in a month o' blue Mondays, if you catch my wind. I mean, you gotta be unflexible enough to cut the next guy some slacks, allow for his undifferentiation, or it'll come back to haunt your ass big time, when you least suspect the worst to pounce into your laps o' luxury, if you catch the draft o' my drift.

But I gotta emit, them mackerel snappers who come into Redbird's every mornin' really is untolerant. They ain't fingered out yet there's other minkeys in the jungle. Truth is, all that Jesus Christ shit can stick in your crawdad, get damn unnoxious. They think he's some kind of unvisible shield protectin' 'em from acrid rain 'n orange agents 'n ADES.

What else they ain't got fingered out yet is that them

Greeks was plenty fuckin' smart sombitches theirselfs, in actualism, long before facks machines, xeroxers, vitamin C, High Masts, 'n runnin' with the papal bulls at Daytona 'n the Isle of Athens. Face it, if all Greeks can do with sheeps is shear 'em, I'd be surprised as hell. What do you think them antique shepherds from Lesbianos 'n Mess-'o-ptomainia 'n Sizzley did up in them cold, misty vales of Arcadelphia on all them lonely nights away from the oasal? You can damn well bet they knew how to keep warm without havin' to wear a wool robe, if you catch my inflockuation, knew all the ins 'n outs, if you catch the push-me o' my pull-you, when it came to diddlin' their flockyouasians and had a right fine time of it, too, if you catch the yens o' my yanks, guarangoddamnteeya. Flockin' A!

Professor Emeritus
of Western Civilization

He has days, lately, months, years, when he can't remember what he's forgotten during these many despondent decades of his deterioration, can't recall his rigorous language training, the memorization of leaders, regimes, dynasties, proliferations of cultures, natural disasters, the capacious history of war, successions of civilizations.

In the morning, he can't even select the correct drawer. When he primes his mind to find socks and pull them over his arthritic toes and ankles, threadbare underwear materializes in his hand and vice versa, frustrating his design; tasks require a pilot's preflight checklist.

Nor can he remember that his social landscape was once populated with people, names and faces he can no longer place; he's unable to register guilt at his lack of recognition or realize that the absence of all human beings testifies to a major malfunction.

Most of his biological systems *do* still function, if considerably less effectively. But whether lying in bed, sitting, shuffling, or gazing in the mirror, he's a stranger to himself. If he could, he'd shake his head in disgust, reprising the phobia that used to assail him: losing one's faculties, which he read about so often in that youthful season preceding his lobotomy.

J.C.'s San Francisco Reverie

Back in '67 and '68, twenty-six years ancient and wise, living two blocks east of the ocean, on 47th, between Cabrillo and Fulton, by Golden Gate Park, frightened each fogenshrouded night by horns moaning like stranded Loreleis, I realized that Vietnam was a nonoption for me and that the Haight-Ashbury/Stanyan Street scene was definitely the least of all other pestilential evils, including death by rice-paddy sniper, slant-eyed land mine or hand grenade, friendly Dow napalm, Agent Orange; initiation into San Francisco State College's radical student movements (which would successfully shut down classes for a week by invading and obliterating the administration offices, causing John Summerskill to cry uncle, abdicate to S. I. Hayakawa, a distinguished semanticist [oh, what a hoot that ironic contradiction in terms was for Huey Newton and his Black Panther group, who rumored Martin Luther King, Jr., was sleeping with Carol Doda and Larry Ferlinghetti in an innocuous, color-blind ménage à trois and who would just as well conduct its own war against the gooks as fight two thousand Bull Connors, five million Mayor Daleys, for the right of one Rosa Parks to sit up front in a Montgomery bus]); or DOA delivery at Our Savior of the Ghirardelli Square hospice, OD'd on hard drugs so ubiquitous neither Timothy Leary, the Beats, nor Fillmore West's Shakespearean cast, consisting of Janis Joplin, Gracie Slick, Jimi Hendrix, and Jim Morrison, let alone the tame Bob Dylan and Beatles, could possibly contemplate the complex ramifications of the universal demon they unleashed (a million times more destructive than Hiroshima's Little Big Man) when they discovered LSD, psychedelic precursor of the silicon chip.

How could I have known, in those brief years, that nothing afterward in my experience would approximate the social excess and regressive immorality mortals, in their grossest moments, are prone to and to which I, a relatively innocent Midwesterner, totally apolitical, a fledgling poet trying to grow gracefully into his impecunious profession, with a modicum of modesty and pride, would be exposed, despite my efforts to keep my eyes tightly closed against the runaway teenagers exploding their veins with laced heroin, cocaine, opium, available at the Presidio, Hyde Street Pier, and in the lobby of the St. Francis, on Union Square and that nothing afterward would ever match that egregious irresponsibility and social dysfunction?

How could I have guessed then that, thirty years later, I'd still be feeling the effects of that fallout, yet be limping, relying on an invisible cane to grope blind through streets I use in getting from home to work at the local winery, where I manage the night shift, making sure no one sabotages the assembly line we use to fill and cork our bottles of Dr. Feelgood, that mystical joy-juice elixir whose grapes old sons-of-bitches like me grow on our memories' vines, pick, crush, and infuse with OPEC additives to expedite their fermentation, so that customers worldwide can imbibe from our Fountain of Youth and fantasize they're sharers of that San Francisco event that evanescently came and went, like the Spanish influenza after World War I, without ever really creating much of a sensation on Wall Street or, for that matter, on Worth Avenue and Rodeo Drive, despite the fact that, these days, all of us baby boomers pretend to recall with clarity those glorious flower-power 60s, which few of us actually savored, who, today, instead of emulating the Grateful Dead, prefer to don mail-order made-in-Korea or -Taiwan Harley-Davidson leather jackets, belt buckles, brassards, boots, paraphernalia produced by the millions on sampans and in cantons for eager American consumption, anything that might smack of the mythical in its symbology, absolutely any trinkets and gewgaws and baubles kids might display to suggest that they too have participated in the primal rites of man- and womanhood, that coming-of-age fantasy through which everyone, at eight, eighteen, or eighty, would like to think he's passed and, in passing, advanced to a higher plane of wisdom, from which we can all pontificate to our children on the dangers of excesses and sloth, siding finally with traditional values, ethics, conformity, and, believe it or not, spirituality, faith in a life-force, God, a monotheistic agent, that ineluctable, ineffable essence that transcends every malevolent element in the universe and ultimately guides us, in our ancient sagacity, to that pinnacle of righteous salvation we achieve when we put away all childish things forever and accept the truth that, despite youth and beauty, each of us, ultimately, must meet our Maker and admit that we really aren't such hot shits but rather are stick figures capable of death and corruption and terrestrial decay, certainly light-years away from flower children running naked forever after in Yasgur's Elysian upstate–New York fields — Woodstock?

Hey, you who've followed these free associations to the edges of their insane logic, don't reject all this diffusive palaver of an inebriated Oedipus out of righteous indignation! Look both ways before you cross the information superhighway! *Cuidado!* Know that each eager generation is sure that its initiates have bested its predecessors', if for no other reason than that age is, by its very nature, the epitome of obsolescence. *Cuidado!* Just remember this simple fact: he who has the fastest car today finds himself beneath the scrap yard on the farthest star tomorrow. Hey, heed me, Macho Man, sister Gracie Slick! Don't be too conceited, haughty, arrogant, pompous, hubristic. You're on borrowed time. Youth is a self-destructing cocksucker, a sycophantish lover, whore, courtesan, odalisque. *Cuidado!* Dying is the cosmic common denominator, the equalizer. I know; I've been around two millenniums already.

Ship of Fools

Laddie, I tell ye true, no more heavily laden with human cargo did e'er an oceangoing cruise liner or refurbished riverboat/barge set sail from its port of debarkation without so much as casting off moorings, clearing the inlet for open water. Aye, matey, such was me fate yesterday, when I followed me nose, me fancy, out of pure curiosity — and a touch of the devil in me, possibly — to the Riverfront Station gambling boat in St. Charles, appropriately named for its stationary nature, that literal stick in the mud, colossal eighth wonder of the modern world, rival of the great Pharos of Alexandria, whose beam, paradoxically, entices strangers to pass through its treacherous admission gates like ships in the night, ghost ships, to be sure, laddie, brigantines, frigates, schooners, clippers, corvettes, all operating with skeleton crews, phantom ships moving through spectral cigarette haze, caravels weighted to the gills with tokens, chips, currency, specie convertible into pirate's plunder, booty the landlubbers always proceed to piss to the sea, whether playing at craps, poker, or blackjack tables or feeding pieces of eight, pesos, pine-tree shillings, florins, shekels down hungry slots of machines whose giddy, inebriated reels spin till the players' heads grow dizzy, distracted from the fact that their buccaneer ship is still mired in irons, the proverbial three sheets unfurled to the swirling winds, flapping uselessly in forced-heat breezes reaching all decks through catacombs of ducts.

Aye, blow me down! What a grotesque confusion of souls engaged in runaway gaming, exposing themselves to instantaneous bankruptcy, foreclosure of second mortgages, divorce's two-horned dilemma of alimony and child support, alchemists all, capable of converting plastic into cash into ashes! Blimy, lad! Those slimy, scurvy bastards! If only I could show ye humanity's lowlifes before your very eyes: profligates, degenerates, reprobates of every variety — throw 'em in the brig! Put 'em in the scuppers with the hose pipe on 'em! Make 'em kiss the gunner's daughter! Let 'em walk the gangplank! Limit their losses to five hundred dollars per session! Oh, those beggars, buggers all, rich and impoverished alike, flying the Jolly Roger from the seats of their pants; that ship of fools a doomed debtors' prison, perpetually beached on the polluted banks of the Missouri. Sinners of the Lord they were, me boy, carrying on like that of a Sunday morn — "riverboat gambling," they've officially named their avariciousness!

Aye, then let 'em sail off the edge, who'd bet their last doubloon the planet isn't flat! As for me, I came to inspect the chaos, not stay or play, and feast at the all-ye-care-to-eat buffet. If I have me say-so, laddie, I'll not let ye step foot aboard e'er in your life, lest ye should discover the worm at the core, spend the rest of your days with Davy Jones.

Aye, shiver me timbers, rattle me bones!

A Mama's Boy

Another evening spent in front of late-night TV . . . another sleazy interlude spent in mindless abstraction between sleep and the next day's somnambulism, watching cheap sex, salacious eroticism, misplaced passion . . . another lecherous exercise in masturbatory fantasy, libidinous excess vicariously witnessed, whose secondhand gratification is an anticlimax to the pleasure principle, a solitudinous act of unimmaculate conception, from whose impossible miracle has always come, as is again the case, his only known issue — his own lonely wishes to perpetuate his stalemated lineage — he a sixty-two-year-old Jew bachelor who never left his mother's side until finally she died, who's never even tried to satisfy his priapic desires by expressing them to another male willing to share the sodomistic approximations of heterosexuality by guiding his innocence into the wild, dense wilderness of moist lips and mouth, lubricated anus, he a hypochondriacal little man never intrepid enough to imperil his health, not even for the thrill of evanescent ecstasy, surely not, for certain not, with the murderous alternative disease these days being AIDS, not just syphilis, gonorrhea, genital herpes, which a witch's draught of drugs might relieve . . . another endless evening viewing pederasty, lesbianism, sadomasochism, bestiality, striptease exhibitionism, sybaritic rites of fellatio and cunnilingus, Dionysian appetites exploded into inebriated orgies, animalistic hissing, writhing, moaning, eventually reduced to pure, blind copulation, joining, like ocean waves, in coital swells or grinding down, like canyon walls, under glacial shifts . . . another futile night of silent, screaming deprivation, with no escape from loneliness, no passage back to a turning point, a specific trauma, from youth, puberty, the womb, upon which he might cast blame, excuse himself by explaining his inhibited ways, behavior that ultimately has rendered him a eunuch, a mealy creature no better than a dung beetle, not even its equal really, who expends his diminished energy watching early-a.m. skin flicks on Cinemax to assuage some egregious deficiency in his psyche, brain cells, DNA, heritage, he the abstemious *heder* boy, mama's boy, the Jew boy his goy schoolmates made their whipping boy, the scapegoat who would, paradoxically, grow up to become neither ram nor lusty, cloven-hoofed goat but rather a rack of lamb turning on a cosmic spit of days, slowly roasting over his solipsistic pit, dripping semen, not grease, into his onanistic abyss.

A Day in the Life of a Nightmare

I start from sleep as though awakening from a dream, a dream of murderous consequence, an illusional shifting of flaking mirrors in which truncated facsimiles of my naked body mock me in ever-realigning postures, here arms pinned to leg joints, there head attached to groin, with fingers, toes, and penis connected to chest as though I were a rutting sow with a litter of twenty-one baby tapirs suckling in the lap of my vegetable luxury, anus-mouth capable of braying like a flatulent ass, my dream a deformed gorgon, a dwarf, cretin, Siamese nightmare, upper half chimera, the other, centaur's hindquarters, joined where reality and reason compete with fantasy and insanity for the same surreal air, my dream a distortion of all truth, Mother Earth's aborted fetus, a hydrocephalic unicorn biting off its horn to rid itself of the pain by forming a drain through which it might disappear into the black universe waiting to mate with its soul.

The amorphous space my psyche occupies this eighth day of the week, in the year of *isn't*, is the dream that surfaced with me from sleep. It surrounds and infiltrates my brain, chokes rational beliefs. An intoxicated savant, I stumble in gutters, talk to myself, translate the subtle soliloquies of debris skittering through the blustery air, read the lips of leaves, steam, crows, ever hoping to escape this grotesque incarceration through an opening in the oneiric zone and awaken into a breath of pure deathlessness.

Hell o' Dolly

When I come into Redbird's, this mornin', to grab a spot o' grub to tide me over 'til lunch, or at least the ten-o'-clock-recess bell at the Saturn plant over to Fenton, when I usually grab a unsuspiculous snort-snack from my flask, left over from the wake-up call I treat myself to each mornin', which I keep hid in a secret department in the lid o' my trusty black lunchbox . . . anyways, when I come slunkin' into Redbird's, I notice them mackerel snappers, seven of 'em, or eight (I ain't sure, they're so stuffed together, like a litter o' possums sucklin' off its mother's udders), is gigglin' 'n guffawin' 'n hissin' 'n kickin', like a mad scientist done give 'em a few dozen squirts o' laughable gas, same stuff the dental hygenie uses when she's cleanin' the tartar sauce 'n plague to keep 'em from eatin' up the teeth, them slappin' each other on the arms, pokin' each other's bellies like a pack o' fagnits instead o' growed-up choir- 'n altered boys from the same pi-nocchial school 'n neighborhood church, and even well into my onion-'n-mushroom eggs omlit, I still can't quite catch the drift o' their orgy 'til I see one of 'em hold up the front page o' the *Post*, with this idiot-lookin' woolly sheep starin' out into a whole world it don't know is lookin' straight back at him or her or whatever in-between creature the paper's tryin' to explain it's become — some sort o' hermafroditical mammal they're callin' a clown named Dolly. Hell! To me a sheep's a sheep no matter what it calls itself, and them things stink to high shit.

Anyways, now I can hear them guys lettin' loose like a giant hot-air balloon that somehow done busted its knotted nozzle, and all that heliumtrope's swishin' out, blowin' scraps 'n people 'n cows away like a toronado, them guys laughin' so loud I ain't sure it ain't cryin', 'til I can overhear this asshole they all call Sid ('cause I s'pose that's his real name) holdin' froth on this new research comin' outten

Snotland, where they got wool sweaters 'n woolen blankets up the woolly ass, whole cuntrysides covered in wool 'stead o' trees — tufts, bushes, plants o' wool, even huts 'n castles whose rooves is covered in wool.

"Can you believe they've actually duplicated a sheep?"

"That's *cloned*, Sid, *cloned*."

"What's the difference? They've copied this sheep in Scotland."

"Yeah, we can read."

"But can you believe the *ram*ifications of this?"

"Jesus, Sid!"

"Yeah, you can get ten for the price of one."

"And if you don't like the way one sheep shits, you can change its babies to do it the way its uncles did it."

"What kind of crazy stuff is that, Sid?"

"Hey, just imagine you're pissed because O.J. got off scot-free. You can take one of his genes and fuse it into the nucleus of another and replicate him; then you can retry his clone with a cloned all-white jury and hang the bastard up by his nuts. That way, you aren't violating habeas corpus and double jeopardy."

"But what if the original O.J. takes off in his bucking Bronco and you never catch him?"

"That's so dumb, Sid! They already caught and tried and freed him, except for the civil verdict. So some doctor, pretending to be doing surgery on him for prostate or arthritis, could suck a few genes out when they give him the gas."

"You guys aren't even close. Just imagine, like they showed in *Jurassic Park*, getting some DNA from a chunk of amber . . ."

"What?"

"Amber — hardened beeswax — a fly got stuck in two hundred million years ago, a fly with a mosquito's stinger that stung a dinosaur, and now you extract that dinosaur DNA from the fly you soften up under a Bunsen burner and pull from the wax and slip that gene into a sleeping sheep, and then she wakes up pregnant and, voilà, she delivers a baby triceratops or stegosaurus."

"Hey, I'm impressed."

"But I thought you were supposed to get identical clones."

"That's correct."

"Then how does a mosquito-fly stuck in beeswax make a sheep look like a thunder lizard?"

"A what?"

"Tyrannosaurus rex to you, Sid. Jesus!"

"Whoa, boys! Slow down! Dolly can only do so much. From what I understand, you've got certain logical predispositions and limitations."

"I'm impressed, Bud. Go on."

"Well, you've got to keep apples and apples in the same barrel; you can't mix rotten oranges with fresh pears, if you get what I'm driving at."

"Not exactly."

"Well, for example, you can go back to Hitler's grave, if you can find it — I hear the Russians used it to do test-tube experiments on Brazilians — and get some DNA from his bones or hair or ashes, but you can't mainline it into O.J.'s mother or sister and expect to get a white baby Adolf, because that would really throw a monkey wrench in the ointment."

"Hold those horses, Bud. You mean if you find a white lady stupid enough to act as a surrogate mother, you could actually get another Hitler? You saying this?"

"Absolutely."

"Well, in that case, I can see a son getting a daughter that's identical to his mother and committing incest with her."

"His daughter or his mother?"

"Sid, shut the fuck up!"

"Jesus, a guy could have his mother for a child?"

"The permutations are limitless!"

"So much for science fiction!"

"Hey, and what if women the world over decided to bring a class-action suit against men, began boycotting sex?"

"Yeah, I follow you. Within a generation or two, women would be reproducing only themselves, not men, and men would disappear."

"That's too absurd for words. Women need men; otherwise, prostitution as we know it, that oldest occupation, would completely die out."

"And you'd have no more strip joints, like Q.T.'s, no more need for porn mags and skin flicks, no more painters doing nudes."

"The paper did say that even if they did make another Hitler . . ."

"Hell, they can make a hundred — a thousand — Hitlers if they get enough orders on the Internet."

"*Excuse me* . . . paper said even if they do succeed in cloning another baby Adolf, they can't guarantee that his brain will be the same. He'll be an exact look-alike, a genetical twin, same fruit mustache and sweep of fag-hair and Nazi swagger stick, but his brain will form different, given the fact that he'd now be growing up in Hoboken or Palm Springs or Rock Island-Moline."

"Yeah, I can see that."

"Yeah, it's even possible the bastard could turn out to be a philanthropist, another Rockefeller giving out dimes to winos."

"You guys remember that stupid joke that was going around just a few weeks ago, the one about the Greeks?"

"Yeah, seems kind of ironic now, doesn't it?"

"Sure does, even if it wasn't too damn funny."

"Yeah, the notion of those Greeks discovering a new use for sheep — wool — meaning that in two thousand years they hadn't got past the possibilities of sodomy. That's so stupid."

"Stupid, maybe, but just imagine, in light of what we now know can be accomplished. Take a lonely, horny shepherd from the Acropolis. He decides to diddle his herd; only, he's got a geneticist doctor friend who tells him for a few thou he'll perform the necessary operation, remove some DNA from his big toe or eyeball or gonad and inject it into a dozen eggs from that many of his flock — the best dozen breeder sheep the guy's got. Now the guy is spared the inconvenience of laying his sheep (which, you've got to imagine, is painful at best), and, voilà, nine months later, out of a baker's dozen of prize ewe sheep come a baker's dozen, all looking just like Sid!"

"That's not too damn funny, Bud."

"Hey, Sid, I was just kidding."

"Not funny."

So, by this time, they got my interest up 'n aroused somethin' big time, 'cause even I can reckelnize this news ain't no small hashed browns. I mean, after all, can you imagine bein' able to clown *anything*, any man or woman or child or venison you might want to, just by grabbin' a snatch o' their USDNA? I bet even now they got some of O.J.'s still in a fridge in one o' them labmatories in Sand-a-Monica. I'd give two weeks' salary at the car plant to lay my hands on a few o' his genes right now, just so's I could get someone to plant 'em in a few leftover eggs from Nicole Stimson's blood samples on one o' them glove-plants in her garden, just to see whether the baby glove'll come out black or white or some shade o' brown.

Jeezus! This stuff's so stupid. Then again, what if there's somethin' to it? Maybe the missus 'n me could make another me to bolt them motor mounts to their frames so's this me can sit home with some brewskies and snooze whenever I damn well please, lay back in my Easy Boy recliner and count clowned sheeps 'til the cows come home, if you catch the whiff o' my barnyard's draft.

Fear and Trembling

"You're just terrified of life, that's all."

Taken at face value, this insight would seem to your average psychiatrist no major breakthrough, no great shakes, rather de rigueur, boilerplate, home free, duck soup, Easy Street, Fat City, SOP, compared with more egregious diseases he might have diagnosed for his patient, nothing to obsess over, no biggie, just your garden-variety phobia — "If you know what I mean," he might say if caught on camera making an offhand remark, one of those occasional, unprofessional faux pas for which you pay the price in spades, or in a rare lighthearted moment away from the "rockets' red glare," to borrow a familiar phrase, while catching his breath between malpractice trials.

Truth is, his flippant diagnosis, expressed more out of fatigue than jadedness with his lucrative practice on 57th and Lex, was picked up by the *National Enquirer* and *USA Today*, highlighted on the "Fleecing of America" series on the *NBC Nightly News* with Tom Brokaw.

"Jesus! All I meant to do was minimize my client's anxiety, give him a modicum of peace of mind, one less thing to process over the weekend, and the media's blown my remarks out of Ebbets Field, into the Bay of Pigs."

"But don't you know that kind of comment is politically incorrect, discriminatory, in violation of all the civil-rights laws since 1965? You can't vilify someone, impugn his good character. After all, a man's reputation is his castle, his ticket to success in his profession and community, his empowerment zone. To label someone pusillanimous is tantamount to accusing him of molesting children, performing heinous deeds of sadism, Satanism, terrorism, acting as a consenting physician in assisted suicides, embezzling Barings' Bank with a single computer, bringing down Wall Street with the mere hint of raising the prime rate. After all, what could be more injurious to someone than a casual allegation that he's a chickenshit?"

"Hey, wait just a New York minute here! All I said to Chicken Little — and be-*lieve me*, it was said in the strictest doctor/patient confidentiality — was that he simply seemed to be terrified of life, nothing more, and not to worry, everything would be all right. He had come to me suffering hyperparanoia, ranting like a banshee, repeating some apocalyptic gibberish to the effect that the sky was falling, that Earth was on the verge of being recycled. I tried to assuage him, but then he began saying stuff like he had to catch a UFO in the wake of the Hale-Bopp comet, that he had five quarters in his pocket to use for the commute, and that he and his flock — Henny Penny, Turkey Lurkey, Goosey Loosey, Piggy Wiggy, Ducky Lucky, Horsey Dorsey, Maui Wowie the Cow, Foxy Loxy, Fertile Turtle, Fred, and a whole panoply of assorted Scientology and New Age freaks, mainly from the Midwest and West Coast — had to jettison their terrestrial containers, or vessels, and it was then that I referred him to the higher-ups — no pun intended. At that point, I feared compromising my position as head of psychiatry at Mount Cedars of Sinai and Zion."

"Ah, so you got frightened too, did you?"

"Well, not exactly. Come on! A man's got to protect his turf, guard against aliens and interlopers and muckrakers and tabloiders like you, who go for the solar plexus, punch below the belt, bite off a guy's ear, pour salt on an open wound, while the referee's got his thumb up his ass."

"So you admit you're afraid."

"Yeah, afraid of even rendering a diagnosis anymore, for fear of offending some ethnic sect, gender, creed, cult — you name it — lobby group, political party, religious schism . . . *Jesus!* A guy can't win for losing, if you know what I mean. It's a scary business out there."

Sepulture in February

Last Wednesday night, an uncommonly warm evening for deep February, the sky let loose such an incontinent fusillade one might have mistaken this location for a war zone, an abyss choking with noxious vapors, hissing, misting. Most of us slept through the deluge, some even soothed by the steady pelting on the roof.

But when I parked, the next morning, on the lot serving my office building, took my assigned slot below the sloping grassy strip separating it from another property, bolted from the car, attaché in my right hand, and started making my way to the door, I froze. As far as my eyes could grope, a desperate, death-defying wriggling was in progress. The surface of the macadam ocean, over which I walked with extreme caution, was a graveyard, a black hallucination littered with worms, thousands of slender, pink annelids slithering, squirming, stretching in painful undulations, as if to reach high ground, creatures routed out of sleep in the inundated earth, dredged up in a mindless scourge, writhing in grotesque silence.

I'd seen this all before, in a perpetual nightmare — a brain tumor never removed — derived from Nazi atrocities I'd viewed in numerous too-graphic coffee-table books, lurid documentaries. You know the ones; you know the victims too: human detritus, dazed, naked, nameless near-skeletons with fear tattooed to their genitals, their ravaged dreams — Jews, Gypsies, syphilitics, homosexuals, religious dissenters, morons, misfits, *Untermenschen*, vermin . . . worms, worms to be exterminated to improve the blue-eyed race, worms shot, gassed, burned to a crisp.

Work that day consisted of a dirty, gray migraine blur. By Friday, the lot seemed perfectly clear of debris, but my ears detected myriad hardened dark-brown knots: blood clots, vermiculate shit crunching underfoot.

Not the Only Gamester in Town

He's a guy who buys his prime time the way the big boys like McDonald's, Anheuser-Busch, Wal-Mart, Archer Daniels Midland play it: by the half- and full-minute TV spot, not scattershot but in a tight pattern calculated to have the most lasting impact on whichever gods and goddesses he might propitiate by such premeditated exposure.

His modus operandi changes regularly, depending upon which side of the gurney he awakens on, which direction the smog is blowing, the season, day of the week, phase of the moon, the red tides' rise, the throbbing of his tail. Few fates have ever accused him of hubris, despite his apparent arrogance. Truth is, he knows from too much experience that existence is a bitch, unpredictable as hell.

Nothing's *ever* been too much for him. He's scalped tickets to Christ's crucifixion, schlepped Pet Rocks and Hula-Hoops at funerals, caused megamergers among blue chips and shifty thrifts, computer and biscuit-/cigarette-makers, failing S&L's and pharmaceuticals; he's brokered wars and broken peace accords from the age of the Greek city-states to the Axis coalition; he's introduced presidents to their mistresses, single-handedly altered the course of history by disclosing his visions to Pharaohs and kings; he's fought Jack Johnson, Floyd Patterson, Muhammad Ali, taken a fall in round one or fifteen as America's great white hope, successfully passed as black, spewing, "I have a dream"; he became the seventh wife of Henry VIII; having eavesdropped on Ptolemy, Galileo, and Einstein, he won the cosmic Nobel Prize for physics.

He makes no bones about notions of predestination, deus ex machina shenanigans, first and final fruits, original sin, absolution, salvation. After all, survival demands every manner of favor, patronage, nepotism, sinecure, dirty trick, chicanery, flimflam, public deception, fraud, jailbreak, plain-daylight robbery, Ponzi scheme, on-the-take caper — whatever it takes to break the back of the enemy.

But recently, he's grown, if not lazy, complacent. His devilish zest for life has lost its edge, that nasty, irascible, in-your-face attitude, that desire to bite his thumb and thrust it at every Montague and Capulet he might goad for fun. Lately, he's been running low on unrighteous indignation, begun to bore himself half to death, let death get the upper hand, beat the hell out of him at his own game.

Ringing in Spring Clichés

Curious how, *to borrow a cliché, an old expression, right before my very eyes*, spring has (oh, here comes another one) *made its presence known* just by its silent arrival, which brings to mind (one more, if you please, *to add* clichéd *insult to* clichéd *injury*) that *Poor Richard's Almanac*-like pithy saying *children should be seen and not heard*.

Indeed, *unbeknownst to me* (clichés seem to be multiplying like the 1001 hats of Dr. Bartholomew Cubbins Seuss, materializing as if *they had minds of their own*, engendered by a sorcerer's apprentice), *spring has sprung*, and *I couldn't be happier*; in fact, I should be handing out cigars as if my imagination were father to nature's *pride and joy*.

Oh, what an *embarrassment of* yellow *riches* the jonquils radiate so close to the ground, and, oh, those crocuses, so delicate and yet resilient to the still-cold nights, and, oh, how sensual the just-budding forsythias, blurring vision *in the eye of the beholder!* These epiphanies! These sweet beatitudes! These amazing graces! These *Baruch Atas*! These invocations! These Hail Marys, apostrophes to God, Buddha, Muhammad, *you name it* (to resort to another hackneyed phrase)!

Just being here to proclaim spring's voluptuousness, the earth's fertile renascence, is, *without exception* (there I go again), *an event of such monumental proportions* (or is it *"magnitude"*?) I'm *at a loss for words*, or almost. Writers are, if you haven't already guessed, capable of translating the ineffable into tropes, similes, and metaphors even *the man on the street* (no *gender bias* intended; *I'll have you know, in all honesty, I pride myself* on *political correctness*) can *relate to*, as though the unlikely links between disparate ideas and objects were *second nature* to our *Homo sapiens* species, that *wise-as-an-owl*, highest-on-the-zoological-ladder ape with a desire to hyperbolize, exaggerate, tell "stretchers" (abusing the use of synonyms is spoken here) . . .

Hey, wait just a minute, here! I've strayed from today's topic of discussion: spring. Perhaps, to wrap up my originally intended panegyric, I should qualify all that's come before *by making a long story short*: *time flies*, folks, and what it's all about is *carpe diem*.*

*For a full discussion of this *earth-shattering* term, see *Brodsky's Handy Thesaurus of Commonplace, Idiomatic, Stereotypical, Slangish, and Colloquial Clichés from Greek, Aramaic, Chinese, Swahili, Hieroglyphic, Hebrew, Latin, Middle Earth, and Extraterrestrial* (St. Louis: Two Tapirs Press, 1994). Brodsky makes *clear as a bell* this old-saw/bromide/triticism/warmed-over-cabbage/réchauffé/cuckoo-word phrase by quoting from the following tracts, treatises, essays, apologias, and tomes:

> "Let's Get On with It" (see Masters and Johnson's *Human Sexual Response*)
>
> "Cut to the Chase" (see *Bonnie and Clyde*, the Keystone Kops, and Captain Ahab)
>
> "The Early Bird Gets the First Worm" (see J. J. Audubon, Adam, and Eve)
>
> "Screw the Foreplay" (see Lorena Bobbitt)
>
> "He Who Waits Masturbates" (see Woody Allen and Pee-Wee Herman)
>
> "You Can Stop Some Other Day to Sniff the Impatiens" (see Drs. Welby, No, Jekyll, and Mengele)
>
> "Corinna's Going a-Maying" (see D. Quixote and Cotton Mather)
>
> "Seize the Day" (see H. Ross Perot and L. Iacocca)
>
> "Practice Safe Sex: Don't Fuck Monkeys or Water Buffaloes" (see P. T. Barnum, Jane Goodall, Dian Fossey, and Republic of Uganda)
>
> "A Rose Is a Rose Is a Rose" (see W. Faulkner and Alice B. Stein-Toklas)
>
> "Tempus Fug-it" (see Buckwheat and the Fugs)

"Let Us Sport Us While We May" (see Pete "Charlie Hustle" Rose and G. H. "Babe" Ruth)

"Grab All the Gusto in the Can You Can" (see Petroleum V. Nasby and Carry Nation)

"Go for the Gold" (see Tonya Harding and the Medellin cartel)

"Be a Mensch!" (see Golda Meir)

"Candy Is Dandy, but Liquor Is Quicker" (see Fannie Farmer, W. C. Fields, and Dylan Thomas)

"Eat, Drink, and Be Merry, for Tomorrow Ye Diet" (see Rush Limbaugh and J. Dahmer)

"To the Quick Go the Victor's Spoils" (see Sen. Edward "Teddy" Kennedy et al.)

"Why Put Off 'til Tomorrow What You Should Have Done Yesterday?" (see George Bush, Amelia Earhart, Evel Knievel, and Karl Wallenda)

"A Bird in the Hand's Worth Two in the Bush" (see R. Tory Peterson and Barbara and Millie Bush)

"Now Is the Time for All Good Men to Come to the Aid of Their Cuntry-women" (see President W. J. Clinton and Newt Gingrich)

"Me So Horny" (see 2 Live Crew)

"Opportunity Never Knocks Twice" (see Leona Helmsley)

"It's Now or Never" (see "Fatty" Arbuckle and Mae West)

"Never Say Never Again" (see S. "007" Connery and Ernst Stavro Blofeld)

"Take the 'A' Train" (see N. Hawthorne)

"Oh, Go Ahead! Nobody'll Ever Know" (see "Tricky Dick" Nixon)

"Walk Softly and Carry a Big Stick" (see O. J. Simpson)

"Uh-buhdee-buhdee-buhdee, That's All, Folks!" (see Porky Pig's valedictory speech, delivered at Pork Chop Hill and reprised at the Bay of Pigs)

There Goes the Neighborhood

There are two new primates in the zoo these days. Their strange presence provides a unique view for visitors of all stripes and hues, from inveterate guests, who love the primal pageantry, to kids in strollers, backpacks, or on the loose. Even to the grounds crew, keepers, trainers, curators, vets, administration officials, board of directors, the entire phylogenetic ascendancy responsible for making the institution function, it's curious how no attraction in the past — not the escape and eventual recapture of snakes, crocodiles, birds of prey nor the rare birth, in a nonindigenous ecosystem, of panda bears, lions, okapis, and rhinos, or the always zany three-hundred-pound baby elephants, guaranteed to evoke glee in any gaping crowd — has ever captured the imagination of spectators to such a voyeuristic degree.

Attendance has doubled in the last month, directly correlating to the pair's arrival and installation in their glassed-in cage and adjoining arbored refuge, where, lately, the brace has been seen loafing, taking walks hand in hand, seemingly reading what appear to be books in the shade of a newly planted sugar-maple grove, micturating, defecating, copulating, apparently unaware of intrigued audiences constantly rushing up to witness immodest bodily acts.

Fittingly, the local newspaper, whose owner/editor in chief also just happens to be a generous benefactor of the zoo, has devoted a daily column to their goings-on, a ploy that, in its third week, has undeniably accounted for a growth in circulation, an increase, across the board, in its advertising rates. In last Sunday's lead article, reprising events of the new additions to the zoo's animal family, a reporter described the acquisition as a "stroke of genius," a "coup," a "windfall," a "godsend," a "strike," a "gusher come in," "perfectly brilliant in conception," "a first for the city, the nation, the global village," "a fitting tribute to the vision of our city's stewards to have exhibited the courage to open such an exhibit."

"After all," the journalist waxed enthusiastically, "who else ever would have sanctioned, let alone thought of the potential benefits and profits accruing from, putting on public display an in-all-ways-compatible — even down to blood type — pair of perfectly healthy, fertile, nude human beings?" Concluding her exuberant adulation, the avid staff writer pounded her chest, proclaiming, "This is surely one giant leap for mankind."

Biographical Note

L.D. Brodsky was born in St. Louis, Missouri, in 1941, where he attended St. Louis Country Day School. After earning a B.A., magna cum laude, at Yale University in 1963, he received an M.A. in English from Washington University in 1967 and an M.A. in Creative Writing from San Francisco State University the following year.

From 1968 to 1987, while continuing to write poetry, he assisted in managing a 350-person men's clothing factory in Farmington, Missouri, and started one of the Midwest's first factory-outlet apparel chains. From 1980 to 1991, he taught English and creative writing at Mineral Area Junior College, in nearby Flat River. Since 1987, he has lived in St. Louis and devoted himself full-time to composing poems. He has a daughter and a son.

Brodsky is the author of thirty-seven volumes of poetry, five of which have been published in French by Éditions Gallimard. His poems have appeared in *Harper's*, *Southern Review*, *Texas Quarterly*, *National Forum*, *Ariel*, *American Scholar*, *Kansas Quarterly*, Ball State University's *Forum*, *New Welsh Review*, *Cimarron Review*, *Orbis*, and *Literary Review*, as well as in five editions of the *Anthology of Magazine Verse and Yearbook of American Poetry*.

ALSO AVAILABLE FROM
TIME BEING BOOKS

EDWARD BOCCIA
No Matter How Good the Light Is: Poems by a Painter

LOUIS DANIEL BRODSKY
You Can't Go Back, Exactly
The Thorough Earth
Four and Twenty Blackbirds Soaring
Mississippi Vistas: Volume One of *A Mississippi Trilogy*
Falling from Heaven: Holocaust Poems of a Jew and a Gentile *(Brodsky and Heyen)*
Forever, for Now: Poems for a Later Love
Mistress Mississippi: Volume Three of *A Mississippi Trilogy*
A Gleam in the Eye: Poems for a First Baby
Gestapo Crows: Holocaust Poems
The Capital Café: Poems of Redneck, U.S.A.
Disappearing in Mississippi Latitudes: Volume Two of *A Mississippi Trilogy*
Paper-Whites for Lady Jane: Poems of a Midlife Love Affair
The Complete Poems of Louis Daniel Brodsky: Volume One, 1963–1967
Three Early Books of Poems by Louis Daniel Brodsky, 1967–1969: *The Easy Philosopher*, *"A Hard Coming of It" and Other Poems*, and *The Foul Rag-and-Bone Shop*
The Eleventh Lost Tribe: Poems of the Holocaust
Toward the Torah, Soaring: Poems of the Renascence of Faith
Yellow Bricks *(short fictions)*
This Here's a Merica *(short fictions)*

HARRY JAMES CARGAS (editor)
Telling the Tale: A Tribute to Elie Wiesel on the Occasion of His 65th Birthday — Essays, Reflections, and Poems

JUDITH CHALMER
Out of History's Junk Jar: Poems of a Mixed Inheritance

GERALD EARLY
How the War in the Streets Is Won: Poems on the Quest of Love and Faith

ALBERT GOLDBARTH
A Lineage of Ragpickers, Songpluckers, Elegiasts & Jewelers: Selected Poems of Jewish Family Life, 1973–1995

ROBERT HAMBLIN
From the Ground Up: Poems of One Southerner's Passage to Adulthood

WILLIAM HEYEN
Erika: Poems of the Holocaust
Falling from Heaven: Holocaust Poems of a Jew and a Gentile *(Brodsky and Heyen)*
Pterodactyl Rose: Poems of Ecology
Ribbons: The Gulf War — A Poem
The Host: Selected Poems, 1965–1990

TED HIRSCHFIELD
German Requiem: Poems of the War and the Atonement of a Third Reich Child

VIRGINIA V. JAMES HLAVSA
Waking October Leaves: Reanimations by a Small-Town Girl

RODGER KAMENETZ
The Missing Jew: New and Selected Poems
Stuck: Poems Midlife

NORBERT KRAPF
Somewhere in Southern Indiana: Poems of Midwestern Origins
Blue-Eyed Grass: Poems of Germany

ADRIAN C. LOUIS
Blood Thirsty Savages

LEO LUKE MARCELLO
Nothing Grows in One Place Forever: Poems of a Sicilian American

GARDNER McFALL
The Pilot's Daughter

JOSEPH MEREDITH
Hunter's Moon: Poems from Boyhood to Manhood

BEN MILDER
The Good Book Says . . . : Light Verse to Illuminate the Old Testament

JOSEPH STANTON
Imaginary Museum: Poems on Art

FOR OUR FREE CATALOG OR TO ORDER
(800) 331-6605 · FAX: (888) 301-9121 · http://www.timebeing.com